UNDER THE GUNS OF PALO PINTO COUNTY

Mary Lou waved at her folks until we were out of sight, then turned to me. "I love you, Clements Barton," she said. "I'll miss them, but I love you more."

She scooted in the wagon seat as close to me as she could and laid her head upon my left shoulder. The next few minutes were the most pleasant of my life. I had a girl who would make a fine wife and a fine mother. I was heading out of Palo Pinto county for good and I was figuring on a new start. Life couldn't have been more promising, considering my past.

"I never gave up on you, Clements Barton. I knew we would marry. I love you too much," she said.

Just as I was about to answer her, I felt her flinch against my arm and sag forward. Then I heard the retort of a gun.

Books by Will Camp

Lone Survivor
Escape from Silverton
Blood Saga
Vigilante Justice
Choctaw Trail

Published by HarperPaperbacks

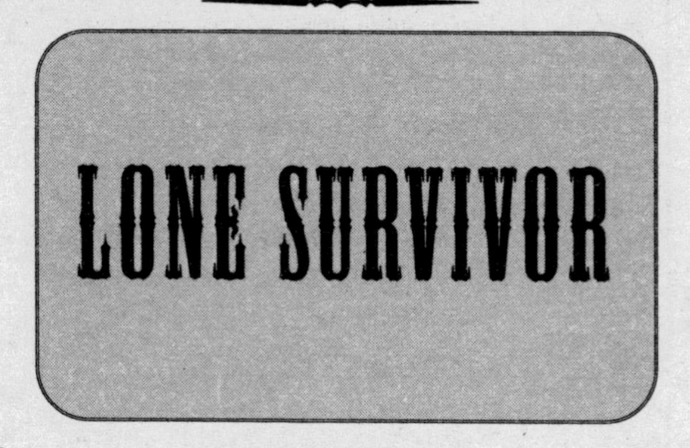

WILL CAMP

HarperPaperbacks
A Division of HarperCollins*Publishers*

This is a work of fiction. The characters, incidents, and dialogues are products of the author's imagination and are not to be construed as real. Any resemblance to actual events or persons, living or dead, is entirely coincidental.

HarperPaperbacks *A Division of* HarperCollins*Publishers*
10 East 53rd Street, New York, N.Y. 10022

Cover illustration by Tony Gabriele

First printing: December 1995

Printed in the United States of America

HarperPaperbacks and colophon are trademarks of HarperCollins*Publishers*

❖ 10 9 8 7 6 5 4 3 2 1

For Jason,
my favorite nephew
and
Lauren,
my favorite niece

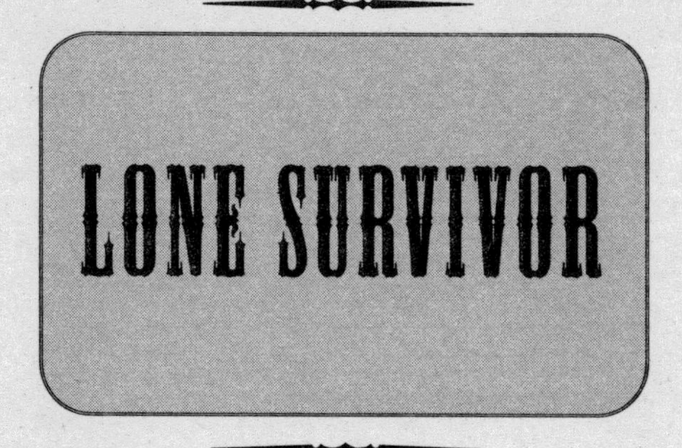
LONE SURVIVOR

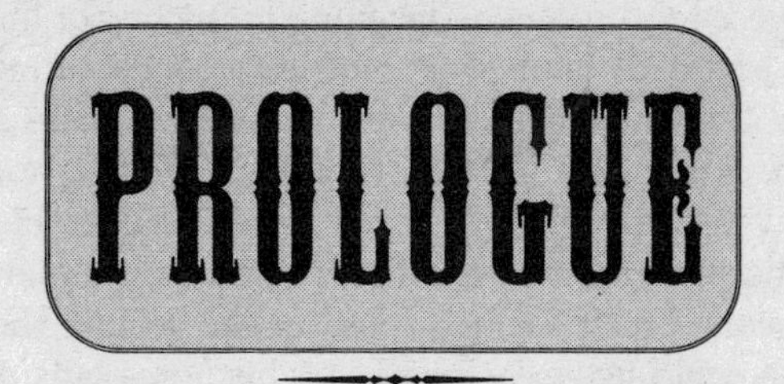

Sliced by the bars of the windows high in the limestone wall, shafts of morning light angled across the warden's office. The thick stone walls were still cool after a long spring night. From outside, the sound of prisoners returning from breakfast and beginning their work details streamed with the light through the barred windows. Seated behind his desk, John Warrenberg, the warden, recognized the grumbles of several prisoners and the hard commands of the guards. A man with a good head for numbers, Warrenberg normally could recite the number of convicts within the prison's stone walls at that moment, or the payroll—to the penny—for the guards who herded the prisoners like surly cattle to their work, or any of the other myriad numbers associated with the details of overseeing a prison.

But, on this morning, just two numbers kept floating through his mind—two and fifty. Two men—Clements Barton and Henry Brooks—separated by fifty years and opposite sides of the law would join him in his office shortly. Warrenberg pulled his pocketwatch from his vest pocket and noted it was 9:45. He held the timepiece for a moment, listening to the tick of the second hand as it bobbed second by second around the face of the watch. He wondered how many ticks of the watch would add up to fifty years. It was a number that even Warrenberg did not care to tackle. He had only been warden of the Texas State Penitentiary for two years, but it seemed like forever despite the fact that he could leave each night for his home outside the walls. Prisoners seldom left except in chains to work the fields, in wooden boxes for the prison cemetery, or in cheap clothes at the end of their sentences.

Fifty was a number Warrenberg could comprehend, but fifty years in prison was a sentence Warrenberg could not begin to imagine. Warrenberg lifted from his desk the prison file of Clements Barton. The file was thin for fifty years of a man's life because Barton had been an exemplary prisoner, even in his youth. There was not a single recorded instance of misbehavior among the papers that documented a half-century sentence for murder. Some prisoners within a week of their arrival at prison had thicker files than Clements Barton had accumulated over his fifty-year term.

Clements Barton had come to the Huntsville prison as the Palo Pinto Kid, the lone survivor of the Barton-Trimble feud in Palo Pinto County. By the time of his capture in 1869, Clements Barton had become an outlaw legend that not even the penitentiary toughs dared challenge.

It took another legend—Texas Ranger Henry Brooks—to finally bring Clements Barton to justice. Now Brooks, long retired, had agreed to come from Austin to witness the release of his former prisoner. Brooks's presence, thought Warrenberg, might prompt Clements Barton to open up and tell the full story of the Barton-Trimble feud. Clements Barton had told no one his side of the story, despite requests from countless reporters and from historians at two universities. Barton's impending release had even drawn requests from the newspapers in Dallas, Austin, Houston, and Galveston for interviews or permission to witness the final meeting between Barton and the warden. Warrenberg had declined them all, and played a hunch that Brooks might trigger Barton's tongue to reveal the story.

Among the hard cases Warrenberg had seen within the prison's walls, Barton's seemed the most tragic. Unlike most of his fellow inmates, he had a conscience, and something seemed to weigh upon his mind. Whatever it was, it must have been a heavy burden to carry for half a century.

Warrenberg straightened the file and placed it on his neatly arranged desk. He adjusted his tie, then tugged each sleeve of his shirt until it showed cuff beyond his coat sleeve. Pushing himself up from his desk, he marched around it to the two chairs where he would seat Brooks and Barton. He patted the two pillows, brought from home, that he had placed in the chair seats to make them more comfortable for the two old men. Then he paced back and forth between his desk and the chairs, wondering whether Clements Barton would survive long in a new century. He couldn't help but feel sorry for the old man who entered prison after the Civil War and would leave it after the Armistice ending the war to end all wars. He shook his head, feeling sorry for the old man, wishing—odd as it seemed—that he didn't have to release him onto the streets at noon.

As the time neared ten o'clock, Warrenberg heard

footsteps approaching his office door. He straightened his coat, cleared his throat, and wondered if he had been right to invite Henry Brooks. At the knock, Warrenberg stepped toward the door.

"Warden," came a guard's voice, "I've Ranger Henry Brooks to see you."

"Retired Ranger," corrected a voice crackling with age.

Warrenberg grabbed the door knob and pulled the door open. In front of him he saw a shriveled old man, his leathery face lined with wrinkles. Except for the granite hardness in his eyes, nothing seemed intimidating about the man, nothing that at one time would have made him feared by outlaws throughout the state. His eyes, though, had a dangerous sheen to them. They were eyes that could wear down another man's resolve. The right hand, which had used a gun so effectively so long for the law, held a cane.

"Mr. Brooks," said Warrenberg extending his hand, "I'm Warden John Warrenberg and I'm honored to meet you."

Brooks offered a tired sigh as he shifted his cane from his right hand to his left. He clasped the warden's hand limply, then withdrew his feeble fingers and ran them through his thinning hair. He said not a word.

"I want to thank you for making the trip from Austin," offered Warrenberg.

Slowly, Brooks nodded. "There's not an outlaw in Texas I'd do this for except for Clements Barton."

The warden gestured toward a chair. "Won't you come in and be seated. Barton will be joining us in a few minutes."

Brooks shifted his cane to his right hand and stepped carefully toward the chair.

Warrenberg instructed the guard to bring Clements Barton to his office in fifteen minutes, then dismissed him. The warden closed the door and marched over to his desk, arriving as Brooks reached his chair, where he hovered for a moment.

The one-time Ranger looked at the pillow, then up at Warrenberg. "I'm seventy-nine, but I ain't that old." With his cane, he knocked the pillow onto the floor, then settled softly onto the hard wooden seat. He planted the cane between his legs, rested his hands on its wooden head, and stared at the warden.

Warrenberg offered Brooks a cigar from the box on his desk.

Brooks shook his head. "Gave up smoking a long time ago."

"Why'd you come?" the warden asked as he put down the cigar box and sat on a corner of the desk.

"I owed it to him. When me and my men captured him, he had a bead on me. He would've killed me if he'd squeezed the trigger. Instead, he threw down his carbine and surrendered. He didn't kill me or anyone else except folks that were in the Barton–Trimble fuss. That told me he was better than a lot of men who are walking free."

"That the only reason?"

Brooks scratched his chin. "I guarded him through the trial and got to know him okay. He was a decent kid. Always seemed to me he got his boot hung in somebody else's trouble and never could shake it free. There was always something sad about him, so melancholy, losing all his family, save his momma. I felt sorry for him and he never treated me but kindly once I'd captured him."

"Did he ever tell you the whole story behind the feud?"

Brooks stared hard at Warrenberg, then spoke softly. "No, sir."

"You think he might talk now?"

Brooks shrugged his feeble shoulders. "I don't think he's got any more reason to talk now than he did before."

"Except to clear his conscience," Warrenberg answered.

The old Ranger looked beyond the warden as if he was staring fifty years into the past.

Warrenberg wished he could have deciphered the old man's thoughts. The warden stared at Henry Brooks, wondering why the mention of the old Ranger's name once struck fear in the hearts of outlaws throughout Texas. But then, it was also hard to believe Clements Barton was once the most hunted man in Texas. And that the moment their lives crossed had been six years before Warrenberg was born.

At the knock on the door, Warrenberg jumped off the corner of his desk. He bent to pick up the pillow Brooks had discarded, then removed the other from Barton's chair. He tossed them on a table under the window, then strode to the door. Out of the corner of his eye, he saw Brooks straighten in his seat.

Warrenberg opened the door expecting to see Barton, not two hours from his freedom, with a smile on his face. Instead, he saw the same emotionless expression Warrenberg had come to expect from the one-time Palo Pinto Kid. Barton, of course, was years from being a kid. Even so, he still seemed hardier than his former Ranger nemesis in spite of the years of prison labor.

Barton, standing in his baggy prison pants and shirt, nodded at Warrenberg. "Warden."

Warrenberg awaited some smile, some indication that this day would be different from each day over the last fifty years, but saw no change in Barton's demeanor. "Come in, won't you? There's someone that's come to see you out." For an instant, Warrenberg thought he saw a glimmer of surprise in Barton's face, but then it was gone like the flame from a dead match.

"I don't have family and I don't have friends. Lost all of those fifty years ago," Barton said trying to look past the warden into the room.

Warrenberg dismissed the guard and stepped aside for Barton to enter. After Barton passed, Warrenberg shut the door, then turned to see Henry Brooks push himself slowly up from his chair. The old Ranger steadied himself with his cane as he faced Barton.

"Hello, Clem," Brooks said softly. "It's been a few years."

Barton blinked, then bit his quivering lip. "Henry Brooks," he managed to say, then bit his lip again.

"I figured a familiar face should be here to greet you when you step outside. It's a different century from when you went in."

Barton's shoulders slumped as he moved toward Brooks. He took the old Ranger's outstretched hand, then hugged Brooks.

Both men seemed to totter for a moment, and Warrenberg stepped toward them, putting a steadying hand on each of their shoulders. Then the two old adversaries seemed embarrassed and broke away from each other.

Warrenberg guided each to his chair.

"I've been outside the walls on work detail," Barton explained to Brooks. "I've seen the changes."

"But you ain't lived them."

Barton let out a long, steady breath. "I quit worrying about living a long time ago. Wasn't much to live for, the way things worked out."

When both men were seated, the warden moved around his desk and slid into his own chair. He tapped the file on his desk and looked at Barton. "Fifty years and not a single problem while in prison. You weren't a troublemaker in prison and never seemed like a killer in the two years I knew you."

"I didn't start out to be a killer. Things just worked out wrong at every turn."

Warrenberg nodded. "Why'd you never tell your side of the story on the Barton–Trimble feud?"

Barton shrugged. "It wouldn't have made no difference."

"Except to clear your conscience," Henry Brooks interjected.

Barton hesitated, as if giving the suggestion a thought.

"There's been reporters, even historians from fine universities, wanting to know what really happened," Warrenberg said.

Barton started to push himself up from his chair. "They're liars, newspapers are. They've written bad things about me before. Now what is it they want to do, strip the flesh from my bones like buzzards?"

Warrenberg shook his head. "Nobody'll be here to bother you. I told them you'd be released tomorrow at noon, instead of today. You'll be gone if any show up."

"Why you doing me any favors, warden?"

"Because you were decent in prison your entire sentence. And I thought you might talk about the feud."

Barton pondered the proposition.

Brooks nodded. "You just as well tell your side, Clem, and get it off your chest. Or it'll be a bur under your saddle the rest of your life."

Barton smirked. "I've ridden with that bur for fifty years."

"Don't carry it with you outside these walls, Clem," Brooks said.

After a long pause, Barton shrugged. "Maybe—as long as you never repeat the story while I'm alive."

Brooks snickered. "I don't have many days ahead of me. You have my word."

Warrenberg nodded as well.

Barton grimaced, then took a long, slow breath and exhaled.

Warrenberg felt Barton's suddenly hard gaze upon him and knew the old man was taking the measure of whether he could be trusted. Barton bit his lips, saying nothing for what seemed to the warden five minutes or more.

"You won't tell nobody, as long as I'm alive?"

"You have my word," Warrenberg replied.

"A man's word ain't always good in prison," Barton replied.

"Mine is."

Barton licked his lips, then took a deep breath. When he began to talk, his voice was soft but steady.

Warrenberg settled into his chair and listened.

Most people've always said the Barton-Trimble feud started over a killing. Nope, it was over something less common than that—a good saddle. By jehu, an argument over a little horse jewelry's what wiped out all the Trimble men and all but me of the Barton men. For some reason, God punished me by letting me live. Of course, the longer I live the less time I'll have to spend in hell with the Trimbles, so maybe God wasn't so bad to me after all.

The Trimbles, though, they didn't expect to wind up in hell, even though I expect that's where I put a couple of them. No, by jehu, they were a Bible-toting, scripture-quoting breed, though there were always stories about Old Man Trimble running around. At every Sunday meeting they ever attended, they'd swear off drinking and dancing—until the next opportunity.

Now, don't get me wrong; I believe there's a God. I spent too many nights on the run with no company but the moon, the stars, the wind, and the varmints He put there. Many a night on the dodge I couldn't sleep because of the mischief of some coyotes yapping or some bobcat screaming or some armadillo rumbling through the brush like a freight train, and me all the time fearing it was some Trimble trying to ambush me or some Ranger trying to introduce me to the hangman. I guess it's only fair that the varmints caused me so much worry because that's probably how God feels about us people when He's resting. We're usually up to some mischief, especially folks like the Trimbles.

I didn't always hate the Trimbles. In fact, Tooter Trimble was the best friend I ever had. They called him Tooter because he had a bugle that one of his brothers brought back from the War Between the States and you could hear him from a mile away blowing on that horn. He never learned to play a tune worth a damn, but he could've blown up a sandstorm over all of Texas with the breath he wasted trying. Of course, Tooter and me were friends before the serious troubles began, but after that I just had my family and Mary Lou Russell.

I was born in 1853 in Benton County, Arkansas, in the northwest corner of the state. My birthday was the last day of December. They named me Clements Barton because Momma was a Clements. I was the last of the brood—eight kids starting with Vernon in 1841, then Nathan, Wilma, Sammy, Charley, Willard, Betsey, and myself.

Benton County bordered Missouri. The border country was mean territory, with people on both sides of the slavery question always at each other's throats. Momma figured bad times were coming, the slavery issue and all of that, and she wanted out of that country. She didn't believe in slavery and didn't believe in politics. Momma just believed in her family and wanted to keep it together. We left Arkansas in 1856 and moved to Palo Pinto County, Texas. Though we moved away from one set of problems in Arkansas, we wound up near another—the Trimbles.

We settled on the Brazos River. It was fair river-bottom land; decent black soil, plenty of good water; and a lot of timber—great cottonwoods, a few pecans, and many oaks. Pa thought we might be able to grow a good cotton crop in the black soil.

We had a decent life until the War Between the States came, then things turned harder with so many menfolk gone. We never had any problems among our neighbors during the war, though I guess we were a clannish bunch. I remember learning about the Comanche depredations and being warned not to wander out of sight of the cabin unless Pa was with me.

"If they catch you," Pa always warned, "they'll skin you, gut you, and cut your head off. Then they'll eat you." I'd seen Pa slaughter and dress hogs, and those words always scared me enough I never wandered too far away. There were some Comanche troubles around Palo Pinto County, though I never saw an Indian.

Early in the war, Vernon joined the Confederate Army. After that, Nathan pestered Momma and Pa to let him go with Vernon. They refused, but Nathan was stubborn. A few weeks after Vernon left, Nathan ran away to catch up with him. He never did find Vernon, but he found the war. When he came home, nine months after the war was over, Nathan was touched in the head; had a puckering scar along the right side of his scalp. Momma, who'd figured him long dead, cried for joy at his return, but something had changed in him. It wasn't the same Nathan. His eyes always looked vacant. He didn't talk much, and when he did it was vaguely tied to the war. If Nathan hadn't run off, or if he'd been killed, the Barton-Trimble feud might never have started. Sammy, Charley and Willard joined the Confederate Army, but just saw a few skirmishes in Arkansas and Louisiana before coming home whole.

I guess we were a lucky family, considering the war, because Vernon had returned at its end, and then, when Nathan showed up with his blank stare, it meant we'd had no casualties. Vernon fought a few nameless battles, but spent a lot of time in hospitals battling some of those Yankee diseases that sapped the strength of General Lee's army. Most other folks we knew who had sent sons to the war weren't so lucky. Most lost one or two, if not all, of their boys. Many families never heard anything from their sons, who just disappeared on battlefields.

It's hard for me to feel sorry for them, but the Trimbles suffered a bad loss in the war. There was nine brothers and a sister before it all got started. Six of the boys went off to war, but the three oldest never returned, one dying in battle in Tennessee, another dying inside a Yankee prison camp in Elmira, New York, and the third just disappearing. Baird Trimble, the oldest surviving brother, was the one who brought Tooter a bugle. I don't know what we'd have called Tooter without that bugle. Hezekiah was his real name. Old Man Trimble and his wife, good Baptists that they were, named all their last six kids after Bible folks. Rumor was Ma Trimble caught her husband sneaking out of a brothel. He found religion real quick after that, naming all his kids for Bible people to prove his faith.

Tooter was my age, and we were best friends until the trouble began. I guess that's what made us such bitter enemies after the pot started boiling. As the crow flies the Trimbles lived up river a mile and a half from our place, but by river distance it was a mile more, the Brazos twisting so.

After the war, Tooter's bugle call often signaled me to meet him at the Rockpile, about midway between our homes. It was an outcropping of boulders scattered about as if God had dumped a sack of stone marbles onto the ground and forgotten to pick them up. There were plenty of places to hide and talk. We had great times there, especially with the river nearby for swimming. It was a perfect place for young boys to play and, a few years later, for bushwhackers.

Just after the war ended, when things seemed to be picking up for us all, is when things began to fall apart. Money was tight. We operated on credit at the stores in Palo Pinto. Vernon, though, didn't take to farming and took up cowboying up north in Jack County. Both he and Baird Trimble, Tooter's brother, went to work on the Four J Ranch. Vernon was able to make a little money and began saving it up to buy a place of his own. Occasionally, he would write home.

One day as fall approached, Pa and the rest of us were out in the field hoeing weeds. Everybody was talking about the upcoming social and dance at Dunker Bend, when Momma comes running and yelling from the house.

"Everybody, come home!" She was waving her apron over her head. "Quick, everybody, come home!"

I thought it must be Comanches, and Pa must have too, because he dropped his hoe and grabbed his rifle, which he always kept handy.

"It's Vernon!" she yelled. "It's Vernon!"

First thing I thought was that Vernon was dead. He wasn't, but he would be within a week.

"He's come home to visit!" Momma yelled.

"By jehu, woman," Pa called out in the throaty growl he always got when he was angering, "either calm down or tell him to write next time so you don't stir up all this excitement."

Pa motioned for the rest of us to resume hoeing, then exchanged the rifle for his hoe. I'll never forget Momma staring at us, then throwing down her apron. Now Momma didn't have many pretty things—nobody did back then—but she always took pride in her aprons. Fact is, when she could drag Pa to Sunday meetings, she'd always wear her best apron. So, when Momma tossed her apron down, she was all rattles and horns.

Vernon came around the side of the house grinning as wide as a barrel, and even from a distance he sure looked good—decent clothes, a new hat and duster. He said something to Momma, waved at us, and took a step toward the field, but Momma grabbed his arm. Then her words came across the distance like an evil omen.

"A man that won't stop his work to greet his oldest son come home brings bad luck to his family."

Momma spun around and pulled Vernon back with her toward the house, leaving her apron there. Pa was in big trouble.

Pa's growl died in his throat, but he kept us hoeing long enough to make us think he was giving up on his own free will. We knew better. Pa was a stubborn cuss, and several of his boys—me included—took after him. In about forty-five minutes, he stopped, plopped his hands atop his hoe handle, rested his chin on his hands, and stared to the west.

When he spoke, his voice lacked conviction and mourned the two hours of daylight he was about to sacrifice. "We've done a good day's work. Let's call it quits, give ourselves plenty of time for cleaning up and supper."

We cheered, then charged for the house, screaming like Comanches. All of us were excited, excepting Nathan. He didn't excite about anything by then and he walked back with Pa. Vernon came out to meet us. He had a shy, almost lonely look about him. I figure he took to the solitary ranch work among men rather than finding a wife because the girl he courted before going to war had died of cholera while he was away. If only she'd lived, maybe he and my brothers would've survived to an old age like me.

"I've got presents for you all at the house," Vernon announced as we reached him.

"Let's go," Betsey answered, tugging his arm.

"Go ahead. I'll wait on Pa and Nathan."

I glanced over my shoulder as I ran to the house and glimpsed Pa picking up Momma's apron, dusting it off, and folding it gently before he greeted Vernon with a handshake. When I reached the house, Momma was setting up the table and ordered me to wash my hands and help. She was still all rattles and horns, so I did what she said.

I was putting tin plates on the table when Pa came up and placed Momma's apron on her chair back. He patted it real soft and turned toward Momma, bent over the cook stove checking her biscuits.

"Vernon's done forgive me, Momma. He knows I'm stubborn."

"No better than me, Joseph Clarence Barton," Momma said, knowing how much Pa disliked being called anything but Joe. As she pulled a pan of hot biscuits from the stove, the aroma tickled our noses. Wilma was carrying pans of potatoes and field corn cut off the cob to the table, and every time she passed, she had one of those female smirks wide across her face, like she was a she-cub taking lessons from her cougar momma.

"I made a mistake. Vernon's forgiven me. Don't make it any worse on me, Momma," Pa said, not particularly pleading, just tired from a hard day's work.

"I'll forgive you, only after you say grace over supper," she answered smugly.

Pa hung his head and nodded. "Okay, Momma, but you know I won't like it." Pa was like me when it came to religion. It wasn't that he didn't believe in a God, just that praying aloud made him humbler in his own eyes, and uncomfortable. A man said his prayers silently. God still heard it, though. Women and those sin-busting stump preachers all figured you had to talk it aloud for the whole world to hear before God could make it out.

By the time Momma called us to the table, she was smiling and humming, but Pa was frowning more than a new steer. The rest of us took seats on the benches, and Momma slipped in her chair at the foot of the table. Then Pa, his head drooping, sank into his chair, crossed his hands, and began to pray without warning.

"Father above," he began, "a man does wrong and his woman scolds him. But without this man and his woman we would have no family. It is good that Vernon has come safely home and we are together. Help this family grow strong and our crops just to grow. And this food, bless it and its humble preparer. Amen."

For an uneducated man, Pa could sometimes be eloquent, at least I thought so, and when Momma lifted her head, her eyes glistened and we all knew Pa had been forgiven.

Vernon broke the uneasy silence. "Now's the time for gifts." He leaned back on the bench and reached for the canvas war bag hanging on a peg on the wall behind us. Putting his hand in the bag, he smiled—he always had such a peaceful, shy smile—then pulled out his fist in front of my eyes. "Didn't have nothing to wrap it with, Clem, so you just unwrap my fingers from around it."

I attacked his strong fingers and discovered beneath them the best-looking pocketknife I ever saw—a three-and-a-half-incher with three blades and a buckhorn handle. I had never received a gift so good. I bet it must have cost 75 cents or more. That was the first time I ever remember receiving a store-bought gift. It was one of the few I ever got. They don't give many gifts in prison.

Vernon gave Pa and all of us boys pocket knives. Then he turned to Momma, Betsey, and Wilma. Out of his canvas bag he pulled three folding silk fans and let Betsey take her choice, then Wilma, and then gave the remaining one to Momma. The girls just giggled when they opened theirs up, and Momma was tearing in the eyes again. "You shouldn't have spent so much, Vernon," she said as she fanned hers apart. The fans were different colors, with gaudy floral patterns and butterflies splattered across them. I thought they were ugly, but they were the type of thing that put the female heart to singing.

"Thank you from all of us, Vernon," Momma said, putting her fan on the table corner. "I'm taking mine to the social on Saturday."

Vernon avoided Momma's gaze. He knew what she was getting at.

Pa saved him for a minute. "Let us eat, Momma. You can pester Vern about the dance while we're helping our plates."

Everyone except Vernon and Momma attacked the sowbelly, potatoes, cut corn, and biscuits.

"The social is Saturday at Dunker Bend. A few folks decided a Saturday away from the crops wouldn't harm much and it'd be a good chance to meet a few of the new families that have moved into the area," Momma said.

Vernon nodded, smiling patiently. "And, there'll be girls there."

Momma flushed, taking the fan, unfolding it, and swishing it in the air. "Maybe it's time you started looking again."

Vernon just whispered, his eyes downcast. "I had a girl. I've still got her tintype. She's the only one I ever wanted."

"There are others," Momma replied gently.

"Yes," Vernon answered, and then began to help his plate.

The rest of us began to eat meekly.

Momma waited a minute, then spoke with resignation. "We're making a day and night of it. Will you go over with us Saturday morning, Vernon?"

"No ma'am," he said quietly. "I'm riding into Weatherford Saturday with Baird Trimble. We're gonna look for a couple saddles."

Momma hung her head, folded her fan, and put it back on her apron. "It'd mean a great deal to me to have the whole family together. Word is there'll be a man there making tintypes. I'd like one of the family."

Vernon nodded. "Sure, Momma, I'll be there—if you promise me you won't push me off on any girls."

Momma nodded as she began to help her plate.

Vernon kept his promise. When he rode up Saturday afternoon, he was sitting atop a brand new saddle.

People from miles around planned to attend the social at Dunker Bend. Most folks called it Dunker Bend because that's where the traveling preacher would hold his sermons once a month when he was passing through. It was a nice bend, with great pecan and oak trees and with plenty of good water for dunking new Baptists.

The Shelby family settled at Dunker Bend and seemed to tolerate the inconvenience of having folks from all over converge on their place. Old Man Shelby—we called him Chicken Shelby because he had more chickens than any man in Palo Pinto County—liked visitors and was tolerably religious. So, he never plowed up the meeting ground or chopped down the trees, just built his home, barn, and chicken coop nearby and enjoyed never having to leave his place for a church meeting or many a social. Chicken Shelby wasn't the best farmer around, but he always had eggs to barter for what he needed.

It was early and the weather was still pleasant.

The cotton crop would come due after the first freeze, and those of us that grew it would be picking cotton until our hands were numb. So, it was to be a good time. It turned out to be the last good time for months in Palo Pinto County.

Early Friday, Vernon had left our place and gone with Baird Trimble to Weatherford. From the moment he left, Momma fretted he wouldn't show up at Dunker Bend. She worried us miserable on Friday, but was in good spirits when we finally left home at good sunlight Saturday. Pa, Momma, Wilma, Betsey, and I rode in the wagon and my brothers rode on horseback, all of us dressed in our best. Momma wore her favorite apron and she and the girls carried their fans.

I was anxious to see Mary Lou Russell. I'd kinda grown fond of seeing her at these socials and at the preachings, but I'd never had the nerve to ask her to dance, me not being much of a talker—or a dancer. Mary Lou was easy on the eyes and as innocent as a newborn lamb. She seemed to take a liking to me—at least that's what my sisters said—and I thought she was prettier than a speckled pup. Now Tooter Trimble had an eye for her, too, and it galled him that she seemed to like me better. The entire ride to Dunker Bend I was nervous, not knowing if she'd want to dance with me. I kept fingering the new pocketknife in my pocket and wondering how much Mary Lou really did like me. I was so nervous, the ride seemed longer than usual.

Folks started gathering about noon Saturdays at these socials, the men talking politics and playing horseshoes and the women fixing a big supper and catching up on gossip. Supper was ready about six o'clock and the dance began about seven and lasted until well after midnight. Everybody'd spend the night sleeping in their wagons or under tarps, and, come Sunday, the traveling Baptist preacher would come and give a sermon, making everybody feel like hell for the good time they'd had the night before and then passing the hat a time or two so all us sinners could buy our way back into God's good graces by bribing the preacher. Sunday was the price the men had to pay for Saturday, but each day seemed to strike a different chord among the women, and they enjoyed them both.

Dunker Bend was about eleven miles upstream from our house, and the road took us right past the Trimble place. I was hoping they'd gotten a late start and maybe Tooter and me could go together the rest of the way, but their place was deserted. So I was left to worry about how Mary Lou would take to my invitation to dance. Since I'd never learned how to dance, thinking it not nearly as important as other activities, I didn't know if Mary Lou would still like me after I'd trampled on her toes and that worried me mightily. I had begun to be interested in girls for a while, but had never been around one before Mary Lou that I liked so. But I was always shy and just didn't know the best way to go about dealing with girls. I didn't figure Betsey, who was a year older than me, and Wilma, who was nine years ahead of me, were good ones to teach me about girls either, them being my sisters. I thought even less of Betsey when she started asking me questions.

"You gonna dance with Mary Lou tonight?" Betsey wanted to know.

I shrugged.

"She'd dance with you," Betsey teased, "because I told her you were a fine dancer." Betsey laughed.

"I can get by," I replied, trying to show Betsey I wasn't going to be intimidated by her teasing.

"But can Mary Lou after you've stepped on her feet?" Betsey laughed.

Pa and Wilma snickered as well, but Momma just looked at them.

Wilma added, "I hope she's not wearing new shoes or you may scuff them, Clem."

Their teasing didn't add to my confidence any, and I let out a deep breath as I shook my head.

"Leave him alone," Momma chided after she saw they'd hurt my feelings. "Seems like the rest of you ought to be interested in finding someone to start a home and family with. I never understood why not one of my children's gotten married yet. Poor Vernon would've been, if cholera hadn't taken his sweet girl."

Maybe us Bartons were just a cursed family. None of us were married, though we ranged in age from twenty-eight as Vernon was to sixteen as I was. We always seemed to know a lot of folks, but I don't know that we ever had close friends. It always struck me odd that the Trimbles, mean as they were, seemed to have more friends than they could shake a stick at and we seemed to be a family of loners.

By the time we reached Dunker Bend, folks had already started gathering and there was a good crowd, including the Trimbles. I looked all around, but didn't see Tooter, so I escaped the howdies and hugging and went out behind the chicken coop to look for him. Not finding him, I went into the trees where we sometimes hid when we were bored with the dancing. I'd just passed a big pecan tree when a shrill blast hit my ear. I jumped and spun around cursing, knowing it was Tooter. He'd slipped from behind the pecan tree and blown his bugle right in my ear.

Tooter was always good at sneaking up on people.

He doubled over laughing. "I scared you good, Clem," he mocked. Tooter was a likable sort except for his pranks.

"You slip up on me again like that and I just might take your scalp," I challenged once I caught my breath.

"If you had a knife, you'd cut yourself, not me," he replied.

"I got a knife."

"Oh, yeah, and I got a rifle."

"I'm not joshing you, Tooter," I said sticking my hand down in my britches pocket and pulling out Vernon's gift.

I could tell Tooter wasn't impressed. He never took it from my palm, just stared at it and shrugged. "Vern get you that?"

Feeling pretty proud of myself and my oldest brother, I nodded. "He did!"

"Well, Baird brought me a single-shot rifle for hunting rabbits," Tooter said, his voice all cocky and full of vinegar.

I felt like I'd been bit by my own dog. I got a knife and he got a rifle. I called his bluff. "I don't believe it. If he bought a rifle, he'd keep it for himself."

Tooter just smiled and stared at me, all puffy like a frog, and I knew he wasn't lying. Tooter was a hefty kid with fleshy cheeks and a thick neck that was easily lost between his head and his shoulders. His lips were sliced thin across his face and his eyes—the right one slightly crossed—were colored the green of stagnant waters. He had a bloated look about him when he bested you at anything, whether it be lying or riding or swimming. And there he was, standing all straight and puffy.

"Then let me see it."

He broke away from me in a dead run. "Only if you can beat me to my wagon!" he yelled.

Well, I knew I could outrace him because Tooter could run all day in the shade of a tree. I took out after him in an easy trot and gained on him even at that. Then, when I saw where the Trimble wagon was, I just picked up the pace and beat him by a good five yards.

By the tailgate stood Ma Trimble, her hands on her hips, just shaking her head at me. "You don't be getting Hezekiah in trouble, now," she scolded me as Tooter lumbered up, huffing and sweating.

"Ah, Ma," Tooter gasped, "he ain't making no trouble."

Ma Trimble just lifted her nose, sniffed the air, and strode off. She was a shriveled-up lemon of a woman, mostly wrinkles and peel with too much of the tart left. It was hard to imagine someone the size of Tooter being the child of that scrawny woman.

Muttering something under his labored breath, Tooter reached into the wagon and pulled out a single-shot rifle that was about the ugliest gun I'd ever seen. He tossed it to me and I studied the Whitney Excelsior single-shot top loader. It was an odd-looking rifle, more stock than barrel, that took .38-caliber cartridges from the top. Though it was uglier than any rifle I'd ever held, it still humbled the fine pocketknife I'd received.

Tooter pulled a carton of cartridges out of the wagon and nodded. "Let's head up river and do a little shooting."

Since I hadn't seen Mary Lou Russell among the gathered folks, I nodded. "As long as I can carry it," I answered, figuring if Mary Lou had arrived, it might impress her to see me toting a rifle about.

We scampered off, and when we got far enough away that we didn't figure a gunshot would cause much concern, we loaded up and commenced to shooting, just wasting ammunition at first, but finally settling in on some target shooting after we came across a downed pecan tree that someone had put a saw to. It made a good target, with its heartwood and its rings. We took to shooting to see who could get the closest to the center.

I could've outshot Tooter with my eyes closed. That was as plain as fur on a bear. Then I noticed something that for some reason I never forgot. My pattern of bullet holes was clustered around the center of the stump. Not Tooter's! His bullets were hitting in a pattern about six inches to the left. I took it that his crossed eye fouled his aim. I put that knowledge in the back of my mind, in case I ever wanted to challenge him to a shooting contest, but I never mentioned it to Tooter because he was touchy about his crossed eye.

But, by jehu, Tooter's aim was always left of center. That knowledge would come back to haunt me one day!

When me and Tooter got back to camp, Ma Trimble was there waiting for us, looking like she's ready to arm wrestle the devil. Her juices were boiling, and they were all sour.

"Where you been, Hezekiah? Wasting your ammunition with Clem Barton?"

"Ma, we's just . . ." Tooter started.

"None of that back talk, boy. You need to respect your elders like the Good Book says instead of sassing the poor old woman that brought you into this world." She looked him over, shook her head, then pointed her finger at his nose. "You got your britches dirty and the man's here to make tintypes." She swatted at him and shooed him to the wagon like she would a toothless dog. Then she turned to me. "Scat!" she called like I was some kind of varmint.

Well, I wandered away looking for Mary Lou Russell. A good crowd had gathered under the shade trees, and the chatter of all the folks and the noise of the children at play had drowned out the sounds of Chicken Shelby's hens. Then I heard a commotion from the road to the north, galloping hooves approaching fast. I stood there wondering what was about to gallop out of the trees when I heard a bellow that only the devil himself or a Trimble could make.

About this time, two horsemen broke into the clear, their mounts neck and neck. It was Vernon, though it wasn't much like him to make such a noisy entrance, and Baird Trimble, who had always been a loud type. They were riding hell-bent for folks and their wagons and probably would've run over someone had Vernon not reined up.

"I win!" shouted Baird Trimble plenty loud for everyone to hear, then jerked his reins savagely. "Even if you did best me on that saddle, I've got a better horse."

Vernon gave a shy smile that made him look as innocent as a schoolboy. His eyes blinked with embarrassment, but I didn't pay attention too long because I envied his new saddle. I'd never seen a prettier piece of horse jewelry. It was of a golden leather, handcarved without blemish. I wanted to ride it bad as a crowd began to gather around Vernon. It had been a while since many folks had seen him, and they were curious how he was getting along at cowboying. Vernon dismounted and stood there howdying everyone and nodding his way around the circle of folks. I glanced over my shoulder and saw just a couple with Baird Trimble, even though he had won the race.

Well, I wanted to get on that saddle and ride Vernon's horse over to the corral by the chicken coop, where most folks were penning their animals. Figuring that might impress Mary Lou Russell if she were watching, I worked my way up to Vernon. Seeing me, he dropped his free arm around my shoulder and pulled me close into him while his bay tugged on the reins wrapped tightly around his other hand.

When Vernon released me, I grabbed for the reins. "I'll take that," I said, working between him and the horse. That was when I saw Mary Lou Russell, her petite smile putting my heart aflutter. Vernon still clenched the reins, but I had one foot in the stirrup and was about to pull myself up into the saddle when he grabbed my shoulder with his free hand.

"Get down from there," he ordered. His voice was icy.

"What?" I cried, thinking at first he was joking.

"Do what I say, little brother, and get away," he commanded, his words taut.

Surrounded by folks, I was humiliated with him ordering me around like that. And, worst of all, Mary Lou Russell had heard it, her smile draining away and her eyes avoiding mine the instant I glanced her way.

"Be quick," Vernon continued. "Get away from my horse."

Angering, I jerked my foot from the stirrup and the bay danced away from me, pulling Vernon with him.

"Easy boy," Vernon said, jerking at the reins and scowling at me.

On the way back home after the social, Vernon said his horse was always edgy after a run, and he feared someone might get hurt if the bay got away from me, but I didn't know that at the time and couldn't have felt lower than if Pa had taken a razor strop to me in the middle of the dance. And all of it in front of Mary Lou. I skulked back to the wagon, wishing I wasn't the baby of the family, wishing I'd get treated like a man.

Momma was in the wagon throwing down bedrolls for her and the girls to sleep on. I clambered in behind her and sprawled out on the nearest bedroll, just watching the leaves twirling on the trees overhead and the clouds gliding by.

"Why's your tail between your legs, Clem? Everything's fine, now that Vernon's here."

I just stared at the sky.

"Don't you nap on me, Clem. With Vernon here I want to get all the family in a tintype."

"I'll be here when you're ready," I said, the gall still bitter in my mouth.

"Did Ma Trimble give you a hard time?"

"Yeah," I answered. I had come to expect a hard time from Ma Trimble, but not from Vernon.

Momma finished and scurried away to collect her family. Eventually, everyone gathered at the wagon. I could hear Vernon talking to Pa, laughing about his new saddle. Seems it was the finest saddle in Weatherford, and both he and Baird Trimble had had their eyes on it. They figured they'd better settle who'd get it between them instead of bidding the price up.

"I flipped a coin," Vernon laughed, "and Baird guessed wrong. He sure was sore about it. That's why we raced into the social like that. He was trying to show me up, but I got a better saddle, a better horse, and better horse sense than him."

Pa grunted. "You just watch out for Baird Trimble. I can't say I trust him."

"He's okay, Pa, to work cattle with, but around people he's blustery as the only rooster in a pen full of hens."

"You still riding back with him to the Four J?"

Vernon laughed. "Yeah, we're meeting at the Rockpile Wednesday morning."

Then I noticed Momma staring at me over the wagon side. "We're ready, Clem," she said, motioning for me to get up.

I crawled out of the wagon and Momma swiped at my hair, then handed me a brush. I toed at the ground as I brushed my hair. When I finished, she studied us one by one.

"My, my, we make a good-looking family," she announced, pointing us toward a clearing where the traveling photographer had set up his equipment in the sunshine. He had a rug on the ground with some furniture around it, and behind that a canvas backdrop with a parlor wall painted on it.

We marched his direction, me trailing the rest because I didn't want to be around Vernon. Funny how one day he gave me a knife and I'm as happy as a bull in a pasture full of heifers and the next day my face is dragging so low I can't see over the top of the grass. To make matters worse, Betsey kept watching me with bedevilment in her eyes. It was plainer than the sun she was figuring to pester me. Her gait slowed until she was beside me.

"Clem," she said.

I held up my hand before she could say another word. "I don't want you a-bothering me."

"Clem," she said, mischief still in her eye, "Mary Lou wants to dance with you tonight. Will you?"

Well, by jehu, I swallowed hard and broke out in a cold sweat. I didn't know how to dance and I was powerfully worried that once she found out she'd have nothing else to do with such a clumsy fellow. But I couldn't let Betsey know that. "Maybe I will, maybe I won't."

Betsey winked. "I've seen how you look at her.

You will!" Betsey laughed, then strode over to the photographer.

I followed and tripped over the photographer's rug.

"Watch yourself, Clem," Momma scolded.

"Yes, ma'am," I replied and waited for the squinty-eyed photographer's instructions. He was typical of his breed, all jabber, talking all the time as he manhandled us into position.

"Now, you must be still!" he commanded Pa. "My exposure takes a while."

"Your what?" Pa replied.

The photographer ignored the question. "You'll look like a ghost if you move."

"I'll look like hell if I don't," Pa answered.

Me and my brothers laughed, but Ma just blushed. "Joseph Clarence Barton," she chided, "such language."

Pa bristled. "I say that today and you get all upset. That loose-tongued preacher'll say hell a thousand times come morning when we're all sitting through his sermon and it won't bother you a bit."

Momma ignored Pa's comment.

When we were all stiff in our poses, the photographer gave a final command. "Be still now."

We did as we were told, and that weasel got behind his camera box and seemed to be there forever. All the time my nose itched so bad I could hardly keep from screaming. Finally appearing from behind the camera, the photographer took a cap off the lens. We stared hard at that glass eye until he re-covered it. "That's it," he said.

Us men were glad to be shed of him, but Momma seemed awfully pleased to have our likeness taken. As we split up, I was nervous as a mouse at a cat social. Mary Lou wanted to dance, and I wasn't sure I could bring myself to do it without help. So, while Pa and my brothers fanned out among the others, I followed Momma, Betsey, and Wilma back to the wagon, where they started cooking their contributions to the evening meal. Betsey kept giving me her knowing look, embarrassing me. She didn't tease me again, as if she knew her silence was a greater torture than her taunts. I'd already been humiliated by Vernon and I sure didn't want Betsey to get the best of me.

Momma ordered the girls to watch the pots cooking over open fires. After a bit, I could smell the aroma of red beans a-simmering and potatoes a-boiling. With the girls busy, I sidled up to Momma and cleared my throat. "Momma," I finally managed to say, "could I see you?"

"You're looking at me Clem," she said, that impatient tone in her voice.

"I mean behind the wagon. It's kinda private."

She stared at me a moment, a frown tugging at the corners of her mouth, then a knowing smile washed that impatient grimace away. She put her arm around my waist and escorted me behind the wagon, me peeking over my shoulder to make sure the girls weren't watching.

Around the wagon, Momma let go and winked at me. "Is it about Mary Lou? She seems to like you."

I felt my face color red. Why was it Momma could always see those things? Must be something in a woman's nature that can read right through a man. "Could you teach me to dance?"

Momma smiled broadly. "It *is* Mary Lou." That was all she said for a moment, then her eyes began to mist and she reached for me and pulled me tight against her.

I didn't know quite what to do. "I'm sorry, Momma," I said and she hugged tighter.

"Don't be sorry, Clem. You're my baby and none of your older brothers have taken much to girls yet, and I was just wondering if I'd raised you wrong."

When she released me, she dabbed her teary eyes with a corner of her apron. "I've work to do, but I'll give you a quick lesson."

I was pleased until I saw Betsey peeking around the corner of the wagon and snickering. Momma saw her, too.

"Get back to work, Betsey," she called. "Clem and I have a few things to do first."

As Betsey stormed off, Momma took my hand in hers and told me to put my other on her waist. I did, all the time wondering how it would feel to hold Mary Lou. Momma taught me a two-step dance. Step, close, step; step, close, step; step, close, step. I picked it up okay, and when Momma was done I was feeling more confident. I went out behind the chicken house after that and practiced by myself, always pausing when some of the men would wander by to tend their horses or heed nature's call.

By the time I came back to the wagon, it was nearing supper time. Folks had fashioned great long tables out of wagon sideboards and had covered them with bowls of hominy, beans, potatoes, and more. Platters were heaped with beef and pork, and one platter was covered with fried chicken. Chickens then were saved for their eggs, but Chicken Shelby had enough that he could spare a couple old ones. I wanted a chicken leg, but I knew they'd never last by the time I went through the line. At the socials, the men went through first and took their fill. Then, everyone else got to serve themselves. There was always plenty of everything except chicken.

There must've been two hundred and fifty folks there, and somebody called on Old Man Trimble to offer thanks. Well, the pompous fool must have prayed for thirty minutes, trying to impress the hungry folks and God with his endurance. I thought I'd starve before he said amen, and then it was a while before the men had served themselves. By the time I got through the line, the chicken was gone. I filled my plate and went to a quilt Momma had thrown on the ground for us.

I finished my meal quietly, all the time looking for Mary Lou but never spotting her, and then went back to the table for dessert. From all the cakes, pies, and cookies, I finally settled on a piece of pecan pie. I was scooping it out of the pan when I felt someone's hand upon my arm. It was Mary Lou.

She was smiling. "I'm glad you're having a slice of that pie. I made it."

"That'll make it that much better. Pecan's my favorite."

"That pleases me," she said, her voice as soft as silk. "It would please me, too, if you would dance with me later."

"I will."

She smiled again and patted my arm. "I shall look forward to it, but now I must help with the dishes." She turned and went away, leaving me feeling about thirty feet tall.

I retreated back to our pallet and ate the pie. It was good, though it had a couple pieces of pecan shell in it that I wasn't expecting, but I'd never have told Mary

Lou that. I went back and had another piece for good measure. When I was done, I took my dishes to Momma and the girls and they cleaned them up, then I helped the men hang lanterns and spread tarps on the ground to dance on.

The musicians started gathering and folks congregated around them and the food tables which were still heaped with good eats for people to graze on throughout the night. Tooter came looking for me after a while, his tail still hanging between his legs for how his Momma had treated us.

"Clem," he said, "how about me getting my rifle and us slipping away to shoot 'coons?"

"Nope, Tooter, I plan to hang around the dance a bit," I answered, certain he would figure out I was interested in Mary Lou.

"Ma didn't mean nothing. It's just her way, Clem."

I grabbed Tooter by the arm. "I know, Tooter. I just want to hear some music, maybe dance a time or two."

I figured Tooter'd want to dance with Mary Lou, but he just shook his head. "Ma says dancing's sinful." He shook his head. "After you're danced out, come to the chicken coop and visit me?"

"Sure, Tooter," I answered, wishing he'd go on because Mary Lou was approaching with her sisters.

She saw me and smiled, then joined the girls who were lining up across the way. Boys were gathering around me, talking in whispers and watching the girls cover their mouths and giggle. When the music began, us younger ones had to wait a couple dances until the older folks had had a few turns on an uncrowded tarp.

Finally, we got our chance and I made straight for Mary Lou and still wound up third in line asking for a dance. My heart sank until I heard her tell each one she'd promised me not only the first dance, but also as many more as I wanted.

Stepping up to her, I took her outstretched hand and, without a word, we stepped out onto the tarp to the strains of "Silver Threads Among the Gold." I was thinking step, close, step, step, close, step until I put my hand on her waist, then my mind went numb. I'd never been that close to a girl. I don't remember stepping on her toes, but I was so weak-kneed I may have. I do remember enjoying the sweet smell of her hair and the soft touch of her hand in mine.

When the music died and we stopped, I realized I hadn't said a thing to Mary Lou, but her smile melted away my worry. "I enjoyed the dance, Clements Barton." She leaned toward me and kissed me lightly on the cheek.

"Me too," I said, enjoying the kiss even better.

"You dance so well, you must want to dance with other girls tonight," she said softly, her hand squeezing mine.

"Not when I'm dancing with the prettiest girl around. I'd like to dance with you all night."

Her hand tightened against mine. "I would like that, too," she said, "but I've been sickly and Momma said I could dance only six and then I must rest. It grieves me greatly not to have more, but I'll give you my final five dances."

"I'd like that, Mary Lou Russell."

We doubled our time together by sitting out alternate dances and talking. And when our final dance was done, we lingered on the tarp, holding each other's hands. This time, I pecked her on the cheek, first time I'd ever kissed a girl. "I'd like to see you tomorrow, sit with you during the preaching, Mary Lou."

"That would make me most happy, Clements Barton," she whispered. Her hands released mine and she backed away a couple steps and smiled. Then Mary Lou turned and disappeared into the darkness toward her wagon. Of all the times I had with her later, that is the vision I always dreamed about, her slowly walking away from me and fading into the darkness.

And then she was gone, so I wandered toward the chicken coop and Tooter. When I found him, he was stumbling around outside the henhouse.

"What took you so long?" he demanded.

I could smell the whiskey on his breath. "I liked the music," I answered.

"You can hear that noise from here. I bet you've been dancing with Mary Lou." He paused a moment, then changed the subject bluntly. "Baird's mad at Vernon for cheating him out of that saddle on the coin flip."

"Vernon wouldn't cheat," I said figuring I ought to defend blood kin, even if I was still mad at him.

Tooter laughed. "I've thought about swapping saddles on their horses. They're both over here tied to the fence."

"Too much work," I answered.

There was this silence. I couldn't really make out Tooter's expression in the dark, but I could smell his breath when he stepped closer to me. "My brothers hid a jug in the chicken coop, told me to keep watch on it. You want some?"

Momma and Pa would've thrashed me good if they knew, but I figured nothing would be harmed by me taking a drink, not with Mary Lou done dancing for the night. He unlatched the door, stuck his hand inside, and pulled out the jug as the nervous chickens flapped and squawked. We managed a couple swigs apiece before slipping the jug back inside with the hens. Occasionally, Baird or one of Tooter's other brothers would wander our way for a little liquor, but me and Tooter wasted more of that jug than we could handle. We began to talk about how bad Ma Trimble was for chastising us and how bad Vernon was for not letting me take his bay to the corral. We weren't thinking straight and we plotted ways to get even with them, the types of things kids think of but rarely have the courage to do. But we were fortified by bad liquor and worse judgment, so we visited the hen house, carried out our plan, and then had some more liquor.

Sitting against the henhouse wall, we were enjoying our mischief, snickering at our daring, and feeling pretty pleased with ourselves when Baird Trimble came by for his umpteenth nip. Retrieving the bottle, he lifted it to his lips, then cursed me and Tooter for drinking so much.

Just as he was hiding his jug back inside the chicken coop, I heard another man approaching. I could just make him out in the darkness. When he spoke, I trembled. "Clem," Vernon called, "you out here? Who's pestering those chickens?"

"Baird Trimble, by damn," Trimble answered. "You stole the saddle I wanted, why can't you leave me be?"

"It was square, Baird, you know that. You seen Clem?"

Baird grunted. "He's here with Tooter, guarding my—" Baird tripped and fell before he completed the sentence. After pulling himself up, Baird ambled toward the horses.

"Clem," Vernon called, "Momma says it's time for you to get some sleep so you'll be awake for Sunday meeting tomorrow."

"Yeah," I answered, bracing myself against the henhouse, hoping I didn't smell of whiskey as much as Tooter.

"I'll check my horse and go back with you," Vernon answered as he marched toward his bay, meeting Baird, who was staggering back toward the music.

I wasn't too alert from the liquor, but in a couple minutes I heard Vernon cursing and knew he was furious.

"Goddam you, Baird Trimble!" he shouted and dashed toward the dancing.

I gave chase as best I could, but tripped over my own legs. By the time I reached Vernon, he was face to face with Baird Trimble and a circle of men had gathered around them.

"That's right, Baird," Vernon challenged, his fists raised. "I'm saying you wiped chicken droppings on my saddle. You're still mad I got the saddle."

My vision was a bit blurry, so I don't know who all was around, but I heard Old Man Trimble and Ma Trimble beside me.

"Didn't do it, Vern, I didn't," Baird answered.

"Liar!" Vernon's voice was angering mightily.

"You don't be calling me a liar!"

I had to stop it and tell what had happened. I stepped through the ring toward them, but somebody pulled me back and held me.

"Before I call you a liar, you answer me one question, Baird Trimble! What were you doing in the chicken coop then?"

Baird mumbled something, then studied the crowd until he was looking toward me. He must have seen his ma and pa, because he never answered Vernon.

"What were you doing at the chicken coop?" Vernon waited.

With his ma and pa there, staunch Baptists that they were, hell would've frozen over before Baird would've admitted he had been drinking by the chicken coop.

"What was it, Baird, you stealing eggs or gathering chicken droppings to wipe on my saddle?"

Baird lunged toward Vernon. "I wasn't around that chicken coop," he lied before his parents, his neighbors, and God.

Vernon shook his fists. "Then I'm calling you a liar, Baird Trimble."

With that, the men attacked each other, Baird still sluggish from his drinking, taking the worst of it until the men rushed in to break it up. When Vernon and Baird were separated, both were bloodied and bruised.

Old Man Trimble grabbed Baird from the tangle and jerked him aside. "No Barton's gonna call a Trimble a liar!" the old man yelled, and advanced a couple steps toward Vernon before calmer men intercepted him.

I wormed my way through the throng of men to Vernon. He was bloodied, though nothing serious. But what I remember most was Nathan. I could make Nathan's face out in the flickering lanterns some men had brought up. His eyes seemed to burn with hatred, and his face, always haunted by the war, seemed eerily distorted. While others helped Vernon, Nathan just stared and spoke to himself, softly at first, then louder, until he yelled. "Why do us boys always get whipped so?"

That was the beginning of the Barton-Trimble feud. What had started out as the greatest night of my life, me and Mary Lou and all, ended as one of the worst. And all of the misery that followed was caused by two fellows wanting the same saddle and two fellows getting into some mischief. All of it over a saddle.

After the fight, Pa decided we weren't staying at Dunker Bend. He and my brothers went to get our horses from the corral while me and the girls loaded up the wagon. Pa wasn't running, it just gave him a good excuse to clear out and miss the Sunday meeting and all that preaching.

As I gathered our belongings, I felt awfully low, knowing I'd not see Mary Lou Russell in the morning. I'd have enjoyed sitting through a long Sunday meeting with her by my side holding my hand. I was moaning my misfortune when I heard my name softly being called.

It was Mary Lou.

"Here by the wagon," I answered.

I could just make her out as she came to me. I wanted to see her eyes, to know what they said, not just to hear her words, but it was too dark. As she approached, I reached out for her and our fingers touched, then entwined.

She moved closer to me, then, for some reason, took a step back, as if I had done something wrong. I moved toward her.

"Momma doesn't know I'm here," she said, "so I can't stay long. I'm sorry about what happened with your brother. Father said you were pulling out tonight, and I'm sorrier still about that."

Her voice was so sincere, I didn't need to see her eyes. I felt so confident that I stepped toward her, but she pushed away from me.

"Clements Barton, I meant what I said about wanting to see you again," she whispered, "but you've whiskey on your breath. I'll not court a drinking man."

Whiskey had already caused enough trouble for one night, and now this. "Don't begrudge me this mistake, Mary Lou. I'll not shame you again, if you give me one more chance."

"I will," she answered, taking my hand in hers and patting it, but not offering me a kiss, not while I had liquor on my breath. "Good night, Clements Barton. I enjoyed the dance."

Then she was gone. I helped pile more of our belongings into the wagon until the men returned with our animals. We hitched up the mules, took our places in the wagon or on horseback, and started for home. The moon was clearing the horizon and it gave us a little light, but travel was still slow. About a mile out from Dunker Bend, the road curved and we came across a camp with a dying fire, a horse staked out in the grass, and a man sleeping on a bedroll. The campsite affected Nathan somehow.

"It's Yankees!" he yelled. "Run for it!" He slapped his horse and galloped down the road ahead of us, screaming all the time, calling out names of men we'd never heard of before.

The racket, of course, startled the sleeping man and he shot up from his bed. "What the hell is it? I've no money. Please don't hurt me," he called.

I'd heard the voice before, but couldn't place it until Pa spoke.

"I thought you saved that kind of language for your sermons, preacher."

"Joseph Clarence Barton," Momma chided, "he was scared half out of his wits by Nathan's craziness."

"Who is it?" the preacher asked, rubbing hard at his eyes to make sense of the commotion.

"It's the Bartons," Pa answered.

"Trouble?" the preacher asked, a trace of relief in his voice.

Pa ignored the question, but Momma spoke up. "Vernon and Baird Trimble had a difference."

"Ah, the Trimbles," the preacher said, his senses clearing up enough to get himself in trouble with Pa. "People like them's helping bring God to this country."

I couldn't make out Pa's face, but it must have burned. "No, preacher, people like you are driving out the God that's already here."

"Pa!" Momma scolded. "That's not right. Preacher, we're sorry we'll miss your sermon tomorrow, but we best get home."

I felt the wagon lurch forward, and we were on the way.

"God bless you," the preacher called out. "All of you," he added as an afterthought.

For a long while, Momma chastised Pa. "You've no manners, no respect for religion."

"I've respect for God, not for religion and not for these sin-busters that ride around the countryside living on handouts and on you women's foolishness."

Momma said nothing else for a good while, and that always made Pa squirm, but he didn't back down, though I know he was miserable.

Sleep was weighing heavy on me by then and I don't remember much more until we got home, where we found Nathan asleep on the floor. After we unloaded our bedding from the wagon and the girls fixed our sleeping places, I collapsed into bed, it still being dark and me as tired as I ever remembered.

Sunday started late for us, me and Betsey being the last ones up and none too happy about that. Pa was trying to persuade Vernon to go on back to the Four J and let Baird Trimble return on his own.

"I told him I'd meet him after breakfast Wednesday and I intend to keep my word," Vernon answered.

"Harsh words passed between you two," Pa said. "You can't trust Baird Trimble or any of the Trimbles."

"You can't run from your troubles either, Pa. I'd just as well face up to them."

Pa only shook his head. "I'm not asking you to run from them, just to put a little more time between them and you. You'll see Baird back on the ranch. That'll be time enough and nobody there'll ever know you had a bit of trouble."

"I'm doing it my way, Pa."

They argued the issue until the day Vernon was to leave, but I noticed they were careful never to bring it up around Momma, so I knew they both considered it serious business.

Sunday afternoon dragged by, me thinking of Mary Lou Russell and wishing I'd had more time with her and that I hadn't been drunk when I last saw her. I was thinking about her when I heard Charley griping.

"Won't Tooter ever outgrow that bugle?" Charley complained.

I shrugged and realized what Charley had said. Then I listened attentively. The evening was right, and I could make out the bugle. Three blasts, a pause, and three more blasts. It was Tooter's signal that we should meet at the Rockpile.

If Momma or Pa had known what I planned, they'd've tanned my behind, but I just had to meet Tooter. What came between our brothers shouldn't come between us. So I slipped away, knowing I'd get in trouble for missing supper, but figuring I'd get in trouble over something else sooner or later.

When no one was looking, I ran out behind the barn and then into the trees. When I was out of sight, I trotted toward the Rockpile. I made the distance in good time and found Tooter more winded from blowing that bugle than I was from the run.

"We still friends?" Tooter called out when he saw me.

"I'm here, ain't I?" I answered.

He smiled at me and then at a mesquite bush, where his Whitney Excelsior was propped up. He walked that way, and I was worried because the only weapon I had on me was my new pocketknife. I tensed to run as Tooter bent down beside the weapon. He spun around and tossed an apple my way. "Thought you might like this, seeing as how you didn't stay for Sunday meeting and dinner."

Catching the apple, I nodded, then bit into it. "Our drinking sure caused a problem last night," I said between bites. "You didn't tell them what we did, did you?"

Tooter shook his head. "And Baird don't remember

a thing about the fight leading up to it." Tooter grinned. "He sure don't remember wiping the chicken shit on Vernon's saddle."

Tooter and me both laughed.

"He just don't want Ma and Pa to know he was drinking," Tooter concluded.

"Is the trouble over or is it just started?" I asked.

"Far as the Trimbles are concerned, it's over. Baird sent me over here to see if Vernon still planned to ride back with him."

"From what Vernon's told Pa, he does. Wednesday morning, he'll be here."

"That'll please Baird. He was upset about the commotion. Pa, though, is still mad and figures there's gonna be trouble."

"You think so, Tooter?" I worked on my apple.

He sort of stared into the sky like he was troubled by it all. "I don't want nothing to come between us, Clem. You're my best friend in all of Texas." He stared hard at me, then lifted his bugle strap over his head and offered his bugle to me. "You take this."

"What? I don't want your bugle."

"No, take it," he insisted. "I want you to have it. Show you I mean it, about us being friends."

I took it from him and realized he'd never let me even blow the damn thing before. Now, here he was giving it to me. I figured I owed him something to seal our friendship, but the only thing I had was the knife Vernon had given me. My hand worked its way into my pocket. I didn't want to give it to him because I could sure use it more than a bugle, but it seemed the right thing to do. I offered it to him.

As he took it, he said, "Friends forever."

I nodded. "Vernon'll be here Wednesday."

"So'll Baird," he replied.

There wasn't much more we could say. We just nodded and went our own ways. That was the last visit I ever had with Tooter Trimble.

I trotted back home and hid the bugle in the barn before heading toward the house. I got there as the girls were clearing the table.

"Where in Palo Pinto County you been, Clem?" Pa asked.

"Just exploring," I answered, knowing my fate.

"If you're not here for supper, you're not going to eat."

I shrugged. I knew the rules and wasn't much I could do about it. Tooter's apple would get me by until breakfast. But I do remember hunger tugging at my stomach that night and me having this craving for pie. Pecan pie! Mary Lou Russell's pecan pie!

The next two days passed quickly in the field, Vernon helping some, but mostly resting at the house, spending his time with Momma. In the evening, he and Pa would pull a bench outside and sit in the evening cool and talk. Me and my brothers—except Nathan, who seemed to float in a different creek from the rest of us—would gather around and listen. They'd talk about men things; how many pounds of cotton we'd pull, how much it would bring, the high cost of land, the speculators who were ruining this country, who had the fastest horse in the county, that sort of thing. But in every discussion Pa'd ask Vernon if he still planned to meet Baird Trimble at the Rockpile come Wednesday morning.

That Tuesday night, Vernon's last night with us, it came up again. "It ain't safe, Vernon, you going out to see Baird," Pa warned, staring at his dirty boots instead of at Vernon.

"I gave him my word. I'm not gonna break it."

"Maybe a couple of us should go with you, just in case."

Vernon smiled. "That might cause more trouble."

"How do you know he'll even show up?"

Screwing up my courage, I interrupted them. "Baird Trimble'll be there."

Both twisted their heads, their eyes hard upon me. They made me edgy, and I looked around, noticing that Nathan was standing behind the bench, listening.

"What?" Pa said.

"Baird Trimble will be at the Rockpile Wednesday morning."

"You seen Tooter? That why you missed supper?"

I grimaced, and he knew I was guilty on all counts.

"Tooter used that bugle to signal you to meet him, didn't he?"

"Yes, sir," I answered Pa, figuring my best manners wouldn't hurt then. "Tooter said Baird didn't remember nothing 'cause he drank too much liquor and was scared to admit it with all those folks around his ma and pa."

Vernon nodded. "See Pa? Baird don't hold no grudge!"

"Baird's one problem. Old Man Trimble, hypocrite that he is, is another." Pa answered. "He won't take kindly to you whipping his boy."

"It don't matter what you say, Pa. I'm still gonna meet him there in the morning."

About then Momma and my sisters walked up with a lamp. "You men aren't gonna keep Vernon all to yourselves tonight," Momma chided.

We moved the bench and the conversation to the

porch and talked later than usual, everybody joining in except Nathan, who lingered nearby in the darkness just outside the circle of light from the lamp. The conversation covered the good times we'd had as a family, and, when we finally went to bed, I never recalled as much happiness.

Come morning, we were all up early as Momma fixed a big breakfast. Vernon gathered his saddlebags, his Winchester, and his duster and left them by the door, then came to the table to eat. After breakfast, we just sat around, continuing our talk from the night before. Nathan surprised everyone by speaking.

"Want me to saddle your horse, Vern?"

"Sure, Nathan, if you want."

Nathan gathered the saddlebags, the duster, and the carbine and headed out for the barn. He was gone a good while—in fact, he didn't come back, but we were having such a good talk that we didn't pay much attention to his absence, since he seldom spoke. Time grew short and Pa grew nervous as Vernon stood up from the table, stretched, and nodded to us all.

"If some of you boys get tired a-farming and want a job, I can get you ranch work, if you're willing to sweat."

Willard and Charley grinned wide like they'd had enough farming.

Vernon shook all the men's hands, then lifted Betsey off her feet and twirled her around a time before kissing her on the cheek. "You watch out for all the boys."

Letting her down, he hugged Wilma, then turned to Momma.

"You take care of the rest of the family. I don't know how you've kept them together so long."

Momma teared up. "I wish some of you boys had

found wives by now, started families of your own. I feel like I've failed as a mother and that my family line and Pa's will end with you kids."

Vernon kissed her, then held her for a moment. "Time will take care of all that," he replied, then stepped off the porch, all of us following him to the corral, never realizing that something was amiss.

I saw Nathan's horse all saddled and ready for riding, but not Vernon's. Maybe Nathan had taken him down to the river to water him.

"Nathan," Vernon called, "I'm ready to go."

We heard no answer.

"Nathan!" Pa yelled, angry or nervous, I couldn't be sure which.

"Maybe I better go look for him," Vernon said stepping toward Nathan's horse.

Pa grabbed his arm. "You stay here. You're safer here."

I didn't follow Pa then. I'm not sure anyone did, save maybe Vernon. Pa and Vernon lingered around the corral, and the rest of us wandered back up to the house, the girls cleaning up after breakfast and us boys trying to figure out where Nathan might've gone. Shortly, Pa and Vernon joined us around the table and Momma served them cups of hot coffee. They just stared at one another silently.

At first, it didn't register with me, but I noticed the coffee cup stop dead at Pa's lips. Then I heard the popping noise from the north. I looked to Vernon, who was suddenly pale. For the first time, the rest of us understood Pa's fears. A cloud of worry shadowed Momma's face. Maybe a dozen shots were fired. That much gunfire was never good news because it meant trouble, not someone on the hunt.

Vernon stood up. "I better go check."

"No!" Pa commanded with a hard voice. "You can't do no good now."

The sounds of a couple more shots drifted our way, followed by the dreadful silence that all of us were afraid to break.

Finally, Pa looked toward the Rockpile and spoke. "Either Nathan or Baird Trimble is dead by now."

After the gunfire, we waited, stunned. Maybe five minutes later, we heard the hoofbeats of a galloping horse. Everyone jumped up from the table, most of us running to see who was coming, but Pa grabbed his rifle and Vernon jerked his pistol.

It was Nathan!

"Oh, he's alive!" Momma called.

Nathan galloped in wearing Vernon's duster, holding his carbine, and slapping the bay with the reins. I remember Nathan's wild eyes and the three bullet holes in the flapping duster.

He pulled up hard in front of us and tossed the reins to Vernon, then jumped off the rearing animal. He pitched the carbine to Sammy, then stared at Vernon.

"You're safe now, Vern. I got Baird for you." He wrestled his arms out of the duster and shoved it at me. "They're after me," he said with labored breath, then dashed for the corral. He mounted his own horse and galloped away.

Vernon's fretful horse, still blowing from the hard ride, fought Vernon for a moment, then calmed. Vernon reholstered his pistol, took his Winchester from Sammy, and started the bay toward the corral.

"You best ride out quick, Vernon," Pa implored.

"And make it look like I did this?"

"You're safer that way."

"It's not right, Pa. You raised me to do the honest thing."

"I didn't know better."

Vern took the bay to the corral. About the time he returned, we heard horses approaching at a dead run. "Here comes trouble!" Pa shouted, levering a cartridge into the barrel of his rifle. At the sinister click of Pa's rifle, Old Man Trimble and two of his sons rode into view, their wild mounts galloping toward us.

I saw Momma herd the girls into the house and felt cold fear crawling up my back as the Trimbles jerked their mounts to a stop almost at our feet.

"Barton," Old Man Trimble boomed at Pa, "we came for Vern!"

"What for, Trimble?"

"Killing my boy, Baird."

"It wasn't Vernon, Trimble."

"I seen it and I know what I seen." Old Man Trimble pointed to our corral. "Why's the bay lathered? You check the duster Clem's holding and you'll find the bullet holes we put there. Just sorry we didn't hit him. Hand him over."

Pa lifted his rifle. "Trimble, what were you doing at the Rockpile? Planning to ambush Vernon?"

"That's no matter. I seen what happened and I intend to get this settled."

Pa pointed his rifle at Old Man Trimble, and I

moved to the side, figuring some more folks were about to die. "Go to hell, Trimble. You're not the law."

Vernon stepped beside Pa. "Mr. Trimble, I'm sorry about Baird, truly am, but it wasn't me that did it. Send for the sheriff and I'll go with him. That's more than fair. That's the law."

Old Man Trimble studied us all a moment, his eyes laced with hate. If Vernon wasn't persuasive, then Pa's rifle was.

"We'll get the sheriff this time, Barton. Next time, we'll get you and yours without the law."

As they turned their mounts and galloped away, Pa whispered at Vernon. "You leaving, like I said you should?"

"No, sir, I'm not running away."

"Then we ought to kill them now. We'll never have this good a chance again."

I couldn't believe what Pa was saying. Pa, though, must've figured what would come of all this and what was the quickest way to end it. All I was thinking was how Tooter and me had promised not to let family differences get in the way of our friendship. Later I would regret Pa not killing them right there, but at the time it seemed too cold-blooded.

The rest of the day seemed to drag by, us not knowing what to expect for Vernon. None of us worried about Nathan because he rode out of our lives that day, returning only for brief moments. Expecting the worst, we gathered, cleaned, and oiled our guns. We drew river water and filled the kitchen barrel in case the Trimbles tried to lay siege to us. Mostly, though, we just waited and watched.

Just about dusk, two riders came up to the house. They rode in slow and unthreatening, tall in their saddles, the sheriff of Palo Pinto County and his deputy. As they neared, we studied the trail behind them, catching no sign of Trimbles hiding there.

Pa and Vernon gave their Winchesters to Sammy and Charley, then stepped out into the dogtrot. The rest of us stood at the windows, watching and listening. Momma fretted like a wet cat.

"Evening, Sheriff," Pa started as the riders stopped.

"This the Barton place?"

"Yes, sir," Vern answered, "and I'm Vernon Barton. You looking for me?"

"That I am," the sheriff said, his voice so low and calm it was hard for us inside to hear. "I've a warrant for your arrest for the murder of Baird Trimble."

"Let me get my horse and I'll go with you," Vernon said, taking a step toward the barn.

Pa stepped quickly in front of him, blocking the way. Instantly, both lawmen had their hands on their sidearms. Inside, Sammy pushed me away from the window and leveled his carbine at the lawmen.

"Sheriff," Pa said, "can I trust you to get Vernon to jail safely? The Trimbles may try to waylay you between here and Palo Pinto. Wait until daylight to take him in. You can stay here."

"My job's to take him in. Tonight. If I don't, there'll be folks out looking for me. The more folks that get involved, the more chances for trouble."

Vernon stepped clear of Pa. "I'll get my horse. He's saddled."

"You stay right there and loosen your gunbelt," the sheriff commanded. "Call one of your kin from inside—preferably the one that's holding the rifle on me—to show my deputy your horse. He'll fetch him."

Pa yelled at me, and I scooted outside. He told me to lead the deputy to Vernon's horse. I headed toward the corral, the deputy nudging his horse after me. I pointed out Vernon's bay. "Need help?"

"I prefer to work alone," he said, pointing to the house. Once I started that way, he got off his mount and went into the corral, going through Vernon's saddlebags looking for weapons. At the house, I stood on the porch with Pa and Vernon in the uneasy silence that stretched between us and the sheriff.

When the deputy rode back leading Vernon's horse, the sheriff commanded Vern to mount up.

"It's gonna be okay, Pa," Vernon said as his hands slowly unbuckled his gunbelt and let it drop.

"Some of us ought to accompany you, Sheriff, just to make sure he gets to town okay," Pa said.

"We'll manage," the sheriff answered.

"You don't know the Trimbles."

"I don't know you either," the sheriff said, then pointed to Vernon. "Step easy to your horse."

Vernon climbed into the saddle, then the deputy rode up and checked him for weapons. When the deputy moved away, I felt a knot in my gut. Vernon was wearing manacles like an outlaw. It didn't sit well with Pa.

Lifting his finger at the sheriff, Pa was simmering with rage. "My boy here didn't kill no Trimbles. If anything happens to him between here and Palo Pinto, I intend to see that you pay."

"Barton, I'll guard him from folks that try to harm him or try to free him. If you try anything, I'll shoot Vernon first, then I'll come looking for you and see if you're as good backing up your threats as you are spouting them."

With that, he and his deputy backed their mounts away from us, then got on either side of Vernon and started back up the trail toward Palo Pinto. As Pa and I watched them disappear into the trees, the rest of the family gathered around us.

"Sammy, you and Charley, saddle up the horses. I'll gather our guns. We'll go after them," Pa announced.

"No!" Momma shouted. "I won't allow it!"

"Saddle up, boys," Pa said, his voice filled with anger. "Willard and Clem, you're coming, too."

"No! No! Not my babies!" Momma cried, my sisters gathering at her side.

"Before this is over it'll involve the whole family, Momma," Pa answered.

Pa strode past the women while me and my brothers hurried out to the corral. We stumbled over each other in the darkness saddling the animals. We didn't have enough horses and saddles for me, so I rode one of our mules bareback. As we approached the house, I heard Pa and Momma in the biggest argument I ever knew of between them. Mostly they tried to keep their major differences from the kids.

"Don't do it, Pa!" Momma was shouting. "You can get him killed! Vernon wasn't worried!"

"Woman," Pa said passing out weapons to us boys, "Vernon takes after you. He don't see the evil in other men. Vernon's in more trouble without us than with us trailing behind him."

"Don't let this tear up our family," Momma begged.

"We don't always have a choice on what happens to our family," Pa said, "but I'll be damned if I'm gonna let the Trimbles run over us. I'd sooner die this minute." In the darkness on the porch, Pa tried to check the load in his carbine. "Woman," Pa said, "you bring out a lamp so we can see what we're doing."

"I will not," Momma answered.

"Dammit, woman," Pa spoke in a tone of voice I'd never heard before, "move or I'll slap you dizzy."

Momma crawled into the house a defeated woman and brought out a lamp, casting a dingy circle of light our way. By then, Momma and Betsey were bawling.

Wilma just stood there in the dogtrot staring at us, her hands on her hips and her foot a-tapping. "You're fools, all of you men."

Then we heard distant gunshots.

"Fools are we?" Pa shouted as he jumped on his mount and kicked its flank. "Your brother may be dead now and you're calling us fools. Let's ride, boys."

We took out after Pa, galloping at first while we were on cleared land, but soon slowing to a lope because of the darkness. The shooting hadn't lasted long and in the night air it was hard to tell how far away it had been.

In the two hours before the moon rose, we advanced along the trail farther than the shots could possibly have come from. Finding nothing, I thought we might be wrong with our misgivings. If there had been a fight, maybe the sheriff and deputy had gotten Vernon safely away.

After the moon rose, we turned around and retraced our tracks. Nobody said much as we headed back home in the moon's glow. We hadn't seen a thing, and I was scared. My mule sensed my fear and turned skittish and hard to handle. As we neared a bend in the road, the mule smelled something and tried to bolt away. Fearing he smelled a Trimble, I wondered if I was about to die in an ambush. I fretted whether the moonlight was a blessing or curse because, though we could see, it made us better targets.

But as we rounded that bend, what I saw made the moonlight a damnable curse. There, not thirty feet from the road, hanging in a shaft of moonlight among the trees, was Vernon.

"Damn Trimbles!" Pa cried out and spurred his horse toward Vernon. He jerked a knife, the one Vernon had given him, from his pocket and stood up in his stirrups, grabbing at the rope over Vernon's crooked head. Vernon swung lazily from the rope, bumping Pa's horse and spooking him.

"Help me, Sammy!" Pa screamed. "Grab his feet! Hold him up in case there's any life still in him!"

Sammy and Charley jumped out of their saddles and grabbed Vernon's boots, but he was so limp we knew it was no good. Vernon was dead.

I couldn't bear to watch any more and moved my mule next to another tree. Vernon, so full of life and trust when he left, and so dead and awkward now, his head twisted to the side, his neck crooked, and his tongue sticking out. I couldn't stand it and threw up what little there was in my stomach.

When I finished retching, I heard Vernon's body collapse into Sammy and Charley's arms. They were sobbing, and I was, too. All this over chicken droppings on a saddle. I couldn't watch as they stretched Vernon out on the ground, Pa slapping at his face as if he might jar him back to life.

Through my tears, a tree nearby drew my attention, my eyes focusing on it for a bit before I realized a piece of paper was tacked to it. I nudged my mule in that direction and froze at what I saw. It was a note. A note tacked there with a pocketknife. *My* pocketknife! The one Vernon had given me. The one I'd given Tooter Trimble for our friendship vow.

I jerked the paper from the tree and then pulled my pocketknife out. Damn Tooter Trimble, I cursed. No, damn every Trimble that ever walked the face of the earth. In the darkness, I couldn't make out the writing. "Pa!" I yelled. "Someone left a message!"

"Damn 'em," Pa answered. "Bring it here."

I rode over wishing Pa'd come to me because I didn't want to see Vernon looking so bad. As soon as I was within reach, Pa grabbed the paper from me. He held it up to the moon, cursed, then reached in his pocket for a match. Flaring the match to life, Pa held it over the paper.

"Bar-tons be-ware," he said softly as he made out the words. Then, "Bartons beware!" he shouted. "Damn the Trimbles to hell!" Pa screamed. "If any of you Trimble sons of bitches can hear me, let's fight it out now and let our womenfolk get the grieving over all at once."

The world didn't answer back.

"Sheriff!" Pa screamed again, "I'll not forget this! No Barton will forget it until you're dead with the Trimbles!"

Pa was crazed, and us boys didn't know what to say. We just listened.

"You boys all with me in this?" he asked, and we all answered weakly, not from lack of support as much as from the sickness within us. "For now, we gotta get Vernon home. Momma'll blame herself for this, and maybe she should, but I don't know if we'd a-saved him had we been behind the sheriff. Don't none of you blame anybody but the Trimbles. We owe them a killing and we owe the sheriff one."

Pa told me to ride double with Will while Charley and Sammy draped Vernon's body over my mule. They tied him down like an animal carcass and we took Vernon home the final time. Momma and the girls were waiting on the porch when we rode in.

"You all okay?" Momma called out, then I heard a cry in her throat. "Oh, Vernon!" she screamed, running toward the mule. Next Wilma and Betsey commenced to bawling. The mule danced away from Momma, but she grabbed Vernon across the shoulders, hugging and kissing him through his shirt.

"They hanged him, Momma. He's not pretty," Pa said.

Up to then, I never thought of myself as much of a fighter. But after hearing the women cry, my juices were boiling and all I could think about was getting even. I thought of Tooter's bugle hidden in the barn and vowed to return it the next day.

Pa and the rest of us dismounted and broke the women away from Vernon. Carefully, we pulled him from the mule and carried him into Momma and Pa's room, leaving him on the bed. Momma stayed up all night with him, cradling his misshapen head in her arms and wiping at the juices that seeped out. Momma and the girls cried all night. Pa tore up some of the porch planks, hammering and sawing them into a coffin. For years, even when I was in prison, any time I heard a hammer and saw I relived Vernon's death.

Come morning, while my brothers started digging Vernon's grave by a tall cottonwood between the cabin and the river, I slipped down to the barn and pulled Tooter's bugle from its hiding place. I squeezed it in my hand and ran to the Rockpile. After I caught my breath, I commenced to blowing on that horn like

Tooter had done all those years. After a couple minutes, I dropped the bugle on a rock, picked up a fist-sized stone, and began to beat it into a useless piece of tin, wishing all the time it was Tooter or one of his brothers I was pounding. When I was done, I left it where the Trimbles would find it, then hid a safe distance away to watch.

In maybe fifteen minutes, I heard Tooter's croaky voice from the brush. "Clem?" he called. "You there?"

I was tempted to answer, then whip the dickens out of him, but I just waited silently. After a while, Tooter appeared and looked around, then his Pa and three of his brothers emerged from the cover of the trees, each carrying a rifle. That shook me, and I scooted deeper into the brush and watched.

Old Man Trimble noticed the bugle first. "Hezekiah," he called, "what's that?" He pointed at the battered bugle.

Tooter ran over to see, then held up his bugle and actually put it to his lips like he thought he could blow it.

"What happened?" Old Man Trimble asked.

Tooter thought a minute, and, when he spoke, he sounded different. When you lie, it always sounds different. "Clem stole my bugle and ruined it."

Old Man Trimble spat at the ground. "Them Bartons is all the same. If you ever get a chance, kill another one like we did Vernon, you hear?"

"Yes, sir," Tooter answered.

I stared through my anger, wondering all the time which one of them had put the rope around Vernon's neck and which had spooked his horse, leaving him hanging there in the night.

When they left, I waited a good half hour before I moved, just to be sure they weren't lurking about. Then

I ran home. It was a somber day for us, Vernon still lying in Momma's bed, Pa working on a coffin, and friends showing up with food and condolences. Somehow, the word had gotten around, and most people arrived expecting a burial that afternoon, but Momma persuaded Pa to wait until the next day. He went along with it to satisfy Momma and to give him a little more time on the coffin. I knew with every stroke of his saw or every swing of his hammer Pa was figuring on getting even with the Trimbles.

I waited around, helping where I could, but mostly just thinking how much trouble a new saddle, the drinking, and the chicken droppings had caused. No matter how much I wanted it, nothing could bring back Vernon or Baird Trimble.

Though a few people had gathered, I didn't feel much like talking, so I wandered among the wagons and camps of those who planned to stay for the burial. I'd made a circle among them all and was walking back to the house when another wagon pulled up. I glanced up into the prettiest eyes I ever saw. It was Mary Lou Russell looking straight at me, a soft smile across her lips. I stepped to the wagon and helped her down while her younger sisters giggled. It felt good to touch her skin and know she was sincere in her delight to see me.

We walked away from the crowd and down by the river, neither of us saying a thing until we were alone.

"I'm sorry about Vernon, but glad you weren't hurt."

I nodded and hugged her. "He didn't deserve to die. He didn't harm no one, just whipped Baird Trimble in that fight at the dance."

"Some folks are saying he ambushed Baird Trimble," she replied.

"Those folks are wrong," I said. "Nathan killed Baird. He took Vernon's horse and duster and ambushed Baird. But Nathan ain't been right in the head since the war."

She gave a little sigh and we stood there a long time, our arms around each other, rocking gently and listening to the river rushing by. After a while, Mary Lou spoke.

"We've known each other for several years. How do you feel about me?"

I loved her, but those were hard words for me to say. "I never wanted to dance with another girl but you."

"Clements, I don't mean to be too forward and unladylike, but do you think enough of me to spend your life with me?"

"I'm thinking I do," I answered.

"Then let's leave, if not now, then after the burial. Make a life somewhere, away from this." Her brown eyes were pleading.

"Away from what? My family?"

"Away from the killing that's coming. It won't stop here. I'll ask you once more to leave with me now. I'll not ask again. Please?"

"I can't," I said. We stood a long time without saying another word.

It was a cloudy day, the day we buried Vernon, like the world was grieving with us Bartons. When everything was ready, several neighbors helped carry Vernon's coffin to the grave. About fifty folks were gathered around, but with no preacher, we didn't know quite what to do. We just stood there a moment, until Stig Russell, Mary Lou's father, stepped forward with a Bible.

He read a scripture and then talked about God accepting Vernon's soul and about compassion and mercy. He asked God to heap mercy on the Bartons, and even the Trimbles, so neither family would suffer another loss. When he was done, I figured I would never hear funeral words more eloquent than his.

Mary Lou Russell stood beside me the whole time, her arm in mine, her head on my shoulder. I noticed an occasional tear sliding down her cheeks. As her pa prayed, she squeezed my arm tightly, like she hoped the prayer for peace would be answered. Then some of the men lowered Vernon into his final resting place.

My brothers helped, but I stayed with Mary Lou until a woman behind us screamed. I turned real quick and gasped. There was Nathan, mounted on his horse, his carbine and reins in one hand, a clump of dried weeds in the other. The mourners parted, and Nathan rode through them to the open grave and tossed the weeds on the coffin. I guess he figured they were flowers and that was how he showed his respect. Like I said, the war sort of turned him loose in the head.

"Nathan," Momma cried, "why'd you do it?"

Pa stepped toward him, anger in his stride. "Get down, Nathan. You as much as killed Vernon." Pa was in a nasty mood, and he rolled up his sleeves like he always did before he'd thrash us with a razor strop.

Nathan recognized the gesture and lifted the carbine at Pa. He mumbled something no one understood and backed his horse out of the crowd. Then he galloped away. After this, stories started circulating in Palo Pinto County about a ghostly rider tormenting people. I always figured it was Nathan, but even he couldn't have done all the things that people blamed on him.

When Nathan was gone and the burial was over, folks started for home. I dreaded the moment Mary Lou would leave.

Her pa came over, hat in hand. "A few more minutes and we best start back, Mary Lou," Stig Russell said, then looked at me. "I'm mighty sorry, Clem, about your brother."

Then my pa walked up and put his hand on Stig Russell's shoulder. "Them was pretty words you said over my boy. I'm plenty grateful and Vernon would be too."

"I wish I could've done more."

"Us men'll do fine. It's the women I'm worried about," Pa said. "They need to get away for a while."

Russell nodded. "They'd be welcome to come with us. It'd be cramped, but we could manage for a week, if you could."

Pa smiled like he had other ideas and turned to me. "That'd be fine. Clem, I want you to go, too, and bring the women back a week from today."

Mary Lou's hand squeezed my arm, and I felt good.

"Mary Lou would enjoy your company, Clem," Stig Russell said. "And me, too, not having a boy of my own."

"I'd like that," I answered.

Pa instructed me to hitch up the team and wagon while he told Ma to pack some clothes and grub for the visit.

"Mary Lou," Stig Russell said, "why don't you help the women with their packing. I bet Clem can work faster without having to keep an eye on you."

I went about my chore and was about finished when Pa came out to the barn. He was carrying Vernon's holster, pistol, and carbine. Handing them to me, he nodded. "You know what to do with these if you have to protect yourself, your mother, or your sisters. Bad times are coming before all this is done."

For the first time, I realized Pa considered me a man, and I felt proud.

"When you're done hitching the team, pull the wagon over to the smokehouse and load a slab of saltpork," Pa said. "I left our last gunnysack of potatoes on the porch for you to take. Any that's left next week, leave with the Russells. Momma's packing some clothes for you in Vernon's war bag. There's a couple boxes of cartridges in there, in case you need them."

Then Pa did something that surprised me more than if he'd pulled a hundred-dollar bill out of his pocket. He walked over, put his arms around me, and hugged me.

"If you want to marry that Russell girl and leave, I'd understand. Momma'd be most happy. Things aren't gonna be too happy around here for a spell," he said. Pa released me and stared me full in the eye.

I should've done it, but I was as bitter about Vernon as Pa. "I'll stay."

Pa frowned. "I figured you'd stay, but Momma wanted me to ask." Then he turned around and marched toward the house.

Watching him walk away, I noticed a sag in his shoulders. I wondered whether it was the years of raising cotton or the weight of revenge that slumped his back. I turned my head away from Pa and toward the cotton field, the bolls beginning to blossom with cotton. It was about time to start picking the crop. It was slow, dirty work, your fingers plucking that wad of cotton from the dried black boll, getting cut and soiled and bloodied. And after a while, your fingers ached when they weren't stiff and were stiff when they didn't ache.

I was glad to be abandoning our cotton field for a spell, until I remembered the route to the Russell place would take us past the Trimbles. After checking the load in Vernon's pistol and carbine, I drove the team out to the smokehouse and got the saltpork, then hurried to the cabin, where Momma and the girls were waiting for me on the porch. Pa came out of the house and pitched their bags in back of the wagon, the girls tossing in extra bedding. Then I helped Pa load the potatoes as the women climbed in and seated themselves.

Stig Russell pulled up beside our wagon. "You ready, Clem?"

With Momma on the seat beside me and the girls settled on the soft bedding in back, I nodded. "Whenever you are."

"Wait, Father," Mary Lou called. "I'll ride with Clem."

Stig Russell grinned as Mary Lou climbed out of the Russell wagon. My own smile was as wide as the moon, and I felt Momma's hand squeeze my arm, like she approved of the fancy between Mary Lou and me. Pa helped Mary Lou into my wagon, and she settled in close to me.

With a snap of the reins, Stig Russell's wagon lurched forward, creaking and rattling like a skeleton on wheels.

Pa stepped off the porch. "You take care of the women, Clem, and remember to be on guard past the Trimble place. If we hear trouble, we'll ride over and clean them out."

"Yes, sir," I said and jostled the reins, the wagon jerking away from the house until the mules adjusted their strides to one another. We drove to the music of the trace chains, everyone in silent worry about what would happen at the Trimble place. It seemed forever to get there, and, as we drew near, I picked up Vernon's carbine from the floorboard and put it across my thighs.

The Trimble place was about fifty yards off the main road, and I recognized the preacher out in front when we drove by. He seemed to be coming to greet us, until he realized who we were. Then he spun about on his heels like he'd seen the devil and disappeared into the house. I looked for Tooter, but didn't see him or anyone else, then laughed to myself about his bugle, wondering if he'd shown it to the preacher.

Tooter didn't scare me, but he had some tough

brothers. There was the twins, Shadrack and Meshack, though most called them Shakey and Snakey. The twins didn't look like twins. Shadrack, or Shakey, was lean and thin like his Ma and had a tremor in his bottom lip. Snakey was a hefty one, taking his name from his like for snakes. He was playing with snakes from the time he was a kid, and would always have one in his pants pocket. I'd heard he even caught rattlesnakes, using them in some religious meetings. The lone girl in the family was Jezebel, or Jessie. She was as sour and as skinny as Ma Trimble and would've been an old maid had she lived that long. The other two brothers were Zachariah, or Zach, and Elijah, or Lige.

We made it past their place without anyone taking up our trail, so we began to talk. In the wagon ahead of us, the Russells were singing a few hymns. Beside me, Mary Lou Russell joined them. She had a voice as soft as a dove's coo. Momma and the girls helped on the songs they knew. I never was much of a singer, figuring a man shouldn't make a fool of himself trying to show he didn't have any talent, but I was a good listener, and it lifted my spirits.

But just before we got to the Brazos River crossing, the singing ended. Two riders approached, and I recognized them as the sheriff and his deputy, the two men who had taken Vernon to his death. They were leading Vernon's saddled bay.

The sheriff greeted the Russells and then came on toward us, a bandage across his head. His deputy, too, had a bandage showing beneath his hat. I patted the carbine resting across my lap. Drawing opposite me, the sheriff halted.

"Mrs. Barton," he said to Momma, with his eyes focused on my carbine, "I'm mighty sorry about what happened to your son. There wasn't much we could do. We did find his horse, but weren't able to find your son in the dark. We're returning his horse to your place. I'm sorry."

Momma just glared at the sheriff, and I watched him shift in his saddle, Momma's silence making him edgy.

"We tried to save him, ma'am, but there's just nothing we could do once we was jumped," the sheriff explained further.

When Momma spoke, there was an edge in her voice as sharp and hard as sword steel. "Deputy, tie the horse to the back of our wagon," she ordered. "Now, Sheriff, answer me a question."

"Anything ma'am," he said, then took off his hat.

"How is it—if you weren't in on Vernon's murder—that when you left our place, Vernon's hands were shackled and when my boys found him there weren't no irons on him."

I was stunned. I hadn't thought of that.

The sheriff stiffened in his saddle and replaced his hat. "The man that got the drop on us forced us to remove them." His eyes stared more at the ground than at Momma or my carbine.

"I don't believe you, nor would my husband," Momma spat back. "Until you can explain it, you best stay off the Barton place.

The sheriff motioned to his deputy, who'd tied Vernon's bay to our wagon. "If I explained it, you wouldn't believe it, ma'am. Like I said, I'm sorry it happened, but if some of your people hadn't jumped us first, he might've lived."

Now I knew the sheriff was lying, because we hadn't left home before we heard the shooting. I moved to lift the carbine from my lap, but instantly I felt Mary Lou's hand pinching tight into my arm.

"That's a lie!" I yelled. "We didn't jump you! We found him hung by the road!"

Mary Lou whispered, "Easy. Nothing'll bring Vernon back now. Good day, Sheriff."

As the sheriff and deputy spun around on their horses and galloped away, I loosened my grip on the carbine and Mary Lou released her hold on me.

Ahead, Stig Russell's wagon moved forward, and I whistled at my mules to fall in behind it. We reached the Russell place a couple hours before dusk, all tired and drained from the trip and the events of the last few days.

Over the next couple days, there were chores to catch up on, and I always helped Mary Lou because she was still weak from her sickliness. Stig Russell seemed pleased that Mary Lou had taken to me. He was lonesome for some male company, and when I wasn't with Mary Lou I was generally with him. Momma and Mrs. Russell made conversation and got along pretty well, and Betsey had Mary Lou and her younger sisters for companions, but Wilma was pretty much alone. Mary Lou would spend time with her, but Wilma was in one of those Barton moods that hung like a storm cloud overhead, generally doing more threatening than raining, but when the rain came it was a flood.

I was out at the barn the second day of our stay, milking the cow for Mary Lou, who was still a bit sickly and needed extra rest, when Wilma cornered me.

"Clem, we best get back home before something happens," Wilma told me, her eyes defiant.

That milk pail was just a-pinging as I squirted white needles of milk against the side. "Nothing's gonna happen here," I answered, disgusted she didn't trust me to protect her.

"Not here," she said. "Back home. The men are without us women to talk some sense into them. They may get themselves killed. Let's go on back! Tomorrow!" There was a pleading in her voice.

"Pa said come back in a week. I'm doing what he says."

She spun around and stormed away, calling over her shoulder, "There'll be hell to pay for all of this, you mark my words."

Maybe we should've gone back, but I knew what Pa had said and Pa had his reasons for everything. They may not have been the best reasons, but I was bound by them.

The day before we were to leave for home, one of Stig Russell's neighbors came riding over. Mary Lou and I were close enough to hear their talk.

"Afternoon," Stig Russell said stretching his arms.

"Stig," he answered, "you heard the news from Palo Pinto?"

"I can't say that I have."

The neighbor leaned over on his saddle, crossing his hands on the saddlehorn and enjoying his secret a moment before he shared it. "The sheriff was murdered!"

Mary Lou took a sharp breath, her hand flying up to her mouth. I straightened up and stared at the rider.

"Yep, sure as I'm a-roosting here, the sheriff was cut down by a rifle blast from the dark. His deputy's hurt bad and the doctor's not sure he'll live."

Stig Russell clucked his tongue. "There's been too much killing lately. They know who did it?" Then he realized Mary Lou and I were listening.

"It was dark, so nobody knows for sure, but most folks think it was those damn Bartons."

I took a step toward him, but Mary Lou caught my arm. "Let it pass, Clem. Don't leave me."

Stig Russell looked hard at the man. "The Bartons are my friends. Fact is, that's their youngest boy over there with Mary Lou." He pointed at us.

The man gave us a quick glance, then nodded to Russell. "Sorry, Stig, just repeating what I heard."

"The Bartons have had a hard time of it the last two weeks," Russell answered. "Let's not make it any worse for them."

The man commented on the fine-looking cotton crop, and Russell gave credit to timely rains. They talked a little bit more about the weather before the neighbor rode on. As he disappeared down the trail, Stig Russell called me and Mary Lou over.

"You two heard what he said, but keep it to yourselves. It's too late for you to head home tonight, Clem, so it can wait until tomorrow. Then you can tell your momma what you've heard."

At supper that night, I toyed with my food, not really hungry. I worried about what I should tell Momma the next day. Mary Lou was good at reading me and left me to my thoughts, except for an occasional pat on the hand.

I've always wished I'd ridden out of Palo Pinto County the next day with Mary Lou instead of going back home. I might've led a decent life with her, but I just couldn't abandon my family.

After supper, Momma was talkative, eager to get back home with Pa and the rest of her sons, but Wilma was still as sullen as a scolded dog, and it galled me, realizing now that we should've left early. Maybe Momma could've stopped things. Mary Lou and I stepped outside and strolled together among the trees, saying very little. I felt her shiver and pulled her closer to me.

"Promise me two things, Clements Barton," she finally said. "You'll not get killed and you'll come back to me."

"I'll be back when this is done," I answered, then turned and kissed her, feeling her tears as they trickled against my cheeks. She shivered, and I wasn't sure if it was from the cold or from fear about the future. "It'll be all right," I reassured her, knowing I couldn't make things all right, but not knowing how else to handle her tears. "We best go in or you'll catch your death of cold."

"Clements Barton," she said, "I love you."

I kissed her again. "I feel the same for you, too, Mary Lou Russell," I replied as we ambled toward the house.

Betsey and Mary Lou's younger sisters teased us as we entered, singing silly kids' poems and calling us lovebirds. Momma winked at me, and I felt my cheeks burning from the embarrassment, but I kept thinking how terrified Momma'd be tomorrow when I told her the sheriff had been killed. Murder was the type of crime committed by mean men, not by us Bartons. We were just farmers—poor ones at that.

Mary Lou was tired and went to bed early. I turned in after that, worried about telling Momma the bad news, about passing the Trimble place again, and about what we would find when we got home. I slept fitfully, and the morning came before real rest caught up with me. I arose listlessly and dressed slowly, waiting until I heard noise in the kitchen to emerge for breakfast. I greeted Momma and Mrs. Russell, who were placing food on the table. Hard bread and cold potatoes did little to restore my strength, though Mary Lou's appearance was a boost.

She smiled coyly at me and pointed to the wall over the stove. "Momma, is that a scorpion?" When Mrs. Russell and Momma glanced that way, Mary Lou planted a quick kiss on my cheek. "I guess it was a shadow," she said when the two women turned back.

Mostly the women talked about the good time they had shared. Momma was cheerful. Even Wilma seemed better, glad to be going home to talk some sense into the men. I drank several cups of that strong Russell coffee to fortify myself. After breakfast, the women gathered our bedding and belongings for me and Stig Russell to load. Downing a final dose of coffee,

I marched outside to hitch the team and saddle Vernon's horse, figuring I'd ride the gelding home and Wilma or Momma could handle the wagon. A chill lay across the land and strong in the air. My hands were stiff with the cold, but I finally got the wagon hitched and Vernon's horse saddled up. I tied him to the wagon and drove up to the house.

Stig Russell was waiting there with an armload of bedding. He smiled, but behind that grin I knew there was worry. "You be careful," he said as he tossed the bedding into the wagon. "I don't know what's gonna happen and I don't want to get caught in the middle of any feuding, but I want you to know there's a place here for you, if you want it."

Crawling down from the wagon, I replied. "You're most kind to offer."

He laughed genuinely. "Mary Lou would make my life miserable if I didn't."

I grinned.

"She's making big plans for the two of you," Russell said scratching his head. "I hope she's not planning more than you are. She'd be mighty disappointed."

I stared at him straight for a moment. "If I ever asked you for her hand, would you let me marry her?"

Without hesitation, he answered. "Yes, sir, as long as you . . . "—he paused—". . . as long as you didn't let her get caught up in any feuding."

"I'll leave Texas if I have to, when the time comes," I said just as Mary Lou stepped outside.

"Time comes for what, Clements Barton?" she asked.

I was at a loss for words. It was easy to discuss my plans with Stig Russell because he was a man. But I had trouble explaining myself to women, excepting maybe my sisters.

"When the time comes for the next social," Russell said, saving me from coming up with a story. Then, Russell went back inside, leaving us alone.

Mary Lou walked over and wrapped her arms around me. "I love you," she said.

"I feel the same for you," I answered.

"Clements Barton," she said, pushing herself away and standing there with her hands on her hips, "can't you say 'I love you' back?"

For a moment, I stammered. She'd caught me off guard and I wasn't so sure if she was mad or just teasing. "I mean it," I said, "but it's just hard to say."

She smiled and returned to my arms. "As long as you mean it. I'll miss you. Will you write me?"

I wasn't much of a writer and figured it'd take a lifetime for me to put something down on paper that was flowery enough to suit what she deserved. Those types of things were difficult for me. "I'm no good with a pencil and paper, Mary Lou. I'd like to, but I don't know what to say, other than I feel the same way for you that you do for me."

Mary Lou laughed. "You really can't say it, can you?"

I felt as foolish as a naked man in church. "Guess not!"

"Can I write you?"

"I'd like that," I answered, "and I'd write you if I knew what you wanted to hear."

"Just about you, that's all."

I nodded. "When you write me, write a sheet on the feelings you'd like me to be writing for you. I'll sign my name to it and add a little about what I'm doing."

Mary Lou just laughed again. "You're still afraid of girls, aren't you? Well, I'm not afraid of you and I'll do it, but you'll be saying things you may wish you never said if you let me put your words on paper."

I hugged her just as Stig Russell came out with the last load for the wagon. He was still grinning when Momma emerged from the house with Wilma and Betsey. Wilma smiled at me for the first time since we had our argument, and Momma was in the best spirits yet. The stay had helped her. The women said their good-bys and climbed in the wagon.

I untied Vernon's bay, mounted, and tipped my hat to the Russells. "Thanks."

"Come back. You're always welcome," Stig Russell answered.

All the Russells waved as Wilma took the wagon reins and slapped them against the mules. I followed them out, and we were bound for home. Glancing back over my shoulder, I saw Mary Lou waving sadly my way. I looked at the wagon, then turned the bay and rode toward Mary Lou.

"You forget something?" she asked.

I nodded and leaned toward her in the saddle. She stepped beside me and stood on her tiptoes, thinking I was going for her lips. Instead, I went for her ear. "I love you."

Mary Lou reached for my hand and squeezed it without saying a thing. The tears in her eyes told me what I wanted to know.

"Do write," I said straightening in the saddle and riding away.

The ride home was a long one, and I didn't know how to break the news. They all seemed so happy, I hated to spoil it. I must have seemed perplexed, because Momma kept glancing at me, her eyes questioning me. Finally, she spoke. "You've been quiet, Clem. What's bothering you?"

"Just thinking," I answered.

"Thinking what?" she replied, a smile on her face like she knew I was dreaming of Mary Lou.

"How I was gonna tell you the sheriff was killed a few nights ago, ambushed in Palo Pinto."

Momma's smile clabbered.

Wilma spit words at me. "I told you we should've gone home before now."

"They don't know who done it," I answered.

"But we do! And, we might've stopped it," Wilma answered with the last words she'd speak before we arrived home.

Momma paled. "We'll ask Pa when we get home. He wouldn't do that." Her words were empty of hope.

I don't understand eternity, but that ride home was as near as I ever came to it. It seemed like it would never end.

When we finally reached the Trimble place, I pulled Vernon's carbine from the scabbard just in case, but the place seemed deserted. Once out of sight, I kicked Vernon's horse into a lope and Wilma slapped the mules, whistling at them to keep pace. When we rounded the last bend in the road and cleared the trees, we saw home.

It was lifeless and strangely different, though I couldn't figure it out at first. Then I looked at the barn and realized some of its lumber had been stripped. Studying the house as I loped in, I realized the windows were shuttered. Pa had torn up part of the barn and built shutters over the windows. The house looked like a fortress. Pa must have figured on trouble.

The house was empty and brooding and the horses were gone from the corral. I rode up to the porch. "Pa!" I yelled. "Pa, you home? Sammy? Willard? Charley? Anybody here?"

Only silence answered. I dismounted, tied my mount to a porch post, and stepped toward the door, the porch wood creaking with each move. Drawing a deep breath, I pushed the door open and slipped into Pa's and Momma's room, checking the corner where Pa kept his rifles. They were gone. Then I knew for sure who had killed the sheriff of Palo Pinto County.

Behind me I heard the wagon stop, Momma and Wilma scrambling out. "Oh my, please don't let this be true," Momma said.

Quickly, I emerged into the dogtrot and checked the kitchen and the other two rooms. All were vacant. "Nobody's home."

"They killed the sheriff, didn't they?" Wilma said.

"We don't know that, Wilma," Momma answered.

"I do," Wilma said pointing to the field. "Nothing's been done since Vernon's burial."

Momma began to sob. As Wilma and Betsey tried to console her, I shooed them inside, figuring the Trimbles, or even the law, might be out in the trees drawing a bead on us. Quickly, I unloaded the wagon, drove it to the barn, unhooked the mules, gave them fodder, and watered them. Then I tended Vernon's bay, brushing him down, wondering all the time where Pa and my brothers were.

There was a lot of work to be done because the woodpile was depleted. Pa and my brothers had wasted no time chopping wood. I grabbed the ax and started working. Momma came out in a while, her eyes still teary.

"Not much need for that, Clem," she said. "Little food's left. Pa and the boys took most of it. They had it all planned. We're gonna have to make a trip to Palo Pinto for supplies. First time in my life I've ever dreaded going to town." She turned, her shoulders slumped and her hands knotted in fists, and moved toward the house.

I carried a couple loads of wood inside to fill the woodbox, then checked the smokehouse. There was plenty of saltpork, so I toted a slab back to the house. By then it was late and I didn't feel like doing anything else. A troubling thought ran through my mind: What if the law thought I had been involved in that shooting in Palo Pinto? It was plenty clear that my Pa and brothers had been.

Momma seemed to be considering the same thing and told me to stay inside, but we were about out of water, so I made several trips to the river, a bucket in each hand, to fill up our water barrel. Come nightfall, we were all quiet and sullen, eating our fried saltpork without a word and finally lighting a lamp when darkness overtook. There's nothing worse than not knowing.

Had we been talking, we might never have heard the squeak of the porch beneath a bootheel. If my eyes got as big as Momma's and Betsey's, then they were the size of wagon wheels. I still had Vernon's gun on my hip, but my carbine was in the next room and there was no way to reach it without going out on the dogtrot. I slipped my pistol out, cocking the hammer and pointing it at the door. The door handle lifted and I took aim for what I figured would be the heart.

"Momma," came a voice from outside.

We all recognized Willard's voice. I lowered my gun as the door swung open.

Momma knocked over her chair as she jumped up and rushed to Willard, smothering him with a hug.

Willard broke away from her. "I don't have much time."

I saw him good for the first time, and his face was scratched and stained with mud, sweat, and dried blood. There was a wild look in his eyes, and in one hand he carried a cocked revolver.

"Pa sent me," he said looking at me. "We're gonna be on the run a while, Clem, and you've got to look out for the women."

Momma reached for his jaw with her trembling hand and turned his face until Willard was looking at her. "Then it's true. You murdered the sheriff."

Willard didn't answer.

"Then it's true, isn't it? You murdered the sheriff?"

Willard nodded. "Just like he let Vernon hang."

Momma began to sob.

"What have you men done?" Wilma demanded. "Blood-letting begets blood-letting. You have torn this family apart." Her words came hot with anger.

"We're not proud of it, but we're not ashamed, either, not with Vernon lying out there cold in his grave. We'll be on the dodge for a spell. Pa says for you not to worry because we'll come back."

And then he turned and disappeared into the darkness before Momma could say anything else. She flung herself into Wilma's arms and they sobbed together, Betsey standing there helplessly as I raced out the door after Willard.

"Willard," I screamed, "wait a minute!"

The only reply I heard was the galloping hooves of Willard's horse. Behind me, I could hear the women bawling. I was scared, and even more so when I glanced toward the Trimble place and saw a light in the trees. A flickering, ghostly light.

My knees trembled and my hands quivered at the thought a Trimble might be out there. I retreated inside, got my carbine, and carried it with me into the kitchen. I kept it at my side from then on, even if I went into the next room.

Betsey was still crying. "We may never see them again," she kept repeating.

I tried to comfort them, but Wilma's iron stare suggested I was to blame for all this trouble. I couldn't look at her without knowing she was right. I couldn't stand her stare, so I left the women to their misery and slipped back outside, studying the strange light, wondering what evil was waiting there for me. I must've stared at it an hour before I finally retreated inside and went to bed as scared as I ever remembered being.

I didn't say anything about the light come morning. Fact was, there wasn't much said that whole day, our spirits being lower than a snake's belly. After dark, I slipped outside and stared toward the Trimble place. My heart leaped into my throat and my knees turned to jelly. The light was there again.

I studied it until Momma called me to eat. I went in and gobbled down my food, convincing myself that I must check it out after super. I tried to stay calm when I got up from the table and picked up my carbine, but Momma sensed something was wrong.

"Going somewhere, Clem?"

"To check the mules," I answered slipping out the door and closing it behind me.

I studied the light a while, took a deep breath, then circled around the house, working my way toward the cover of the trees. Quickly, I was among them, the rustling wind accompanying me and sending chills down my spine. I worked my way slowly toward the light, taking maybe thirty minutes or more to close in on it. Finally, I could almost make it out. I knew it was a fire, but I couldn't see much in the clearing around it. Moving from tree to tree, I reached one as close to the fire as I dared, caught my breath, and peeked around the side.

Then I heard the snap of a twig behind me. As I spun about, I felt a strong hand cover my mouth and another grab me around the chest and pull me away from the tree. I tried to scream, but I couldn't breathe. The carbine tumbled from my hands onto the ground and my arms were pinned, so I couldn't get my sidearm.

I felt the hot breath of my attacker on my neck. I knew I was dead.

I'd let someone slip up on me. I struggled against the iron arm around my chest and the rough palm over my mouth, trying to bite a chunk out of that hand. But the hand pressed against my jaw and nose until my teeth hurt. I wondered which Trimble would take credit for killing me.

"Clem," my assailant whispered, and I smelled the bile of poor food upon his breath. Through the terror clouding my mind, I didn't recognize the voice at first. When I did, it was like I'd been hit by a runaway locomotive. I would've collapsed on the ground from shock except for the strong arms holding me up.

It was Nathan.

"Clem," he whispered, "be quiet and I'll loose you."

I nodded my head against his palm, awed by his strength. Slowly, he released me. I squatted to pick up my carbine, then looked up at Nathan. "What are you doing? You don't know the trouble you've caused." I straightened up, brushing off the weapon and moving toward the fire, hoping Nathan would follow and I could get a look into his eyes.

"Stay," he said, his voice sullen and defiant.

"What are you doing here, Nathan?"

"Guarding the house from those Yankee Trimbles. When you see fire, I'll be guarding you like the army."

"The Trimbles aren't Yankees. Why'd you kill Baird Trimble?"

"He whupped Vernon at the dance."

"Who shot first at the Rockpile?" I asked, hoping that the Trimbles had tried to ambush him.

"I did. Now you go home. I'll guard the house. On nights you see fire burning in the trees, you'll know I'm here. No worry 'bout Yankee Trimbles. I'll keep them away. Now go. Don't tell Momma 'bout me. I've done shamed her enough. Go, Clem."

"Take care of yourself, Nathan," I said, then stumbled back toward the house in the dark.

"What took you so long, Clem?" Momma asked as soon as I got inside.

I didn't answer.

Wilma responded for me. "He's probably out hunting Trimbles, just like the other men in this family. Just like animals."

"Shut up, Wilma," I ordered as I propped my carbine against the wall.

"No." Wilma fired back. "It's time some of you men listened. This killing'll get you nowhere. It won't bring Vernon back and it'll just put more of you in graves. Nathan's gone plum loco and disappeared. Who knows where Pa and the rest of the boys are after killing the sheriff. When'll it end?"

"How'd you handle it then, Wilma, seeing as you know so much?"

Momma stepped between us. "Quit it. We've had enough problems without us fighting among ourselves."

Wilma stormed out into the dogtrot and slammed the door.

"She's upset like the rest of us," Momma said. "I wish she wouldn't be so headstrong like Pa and would find her a man. But she's too stubborn to put up with a man with many faults, and there aren't many men without them."

"Or women," I said.

"Least women aren't likely to kill one another," she said, then broke into tears and rushed across the room, her hands outstretched. She pulled me tight into her bosom.

"I'm sorry, Clem," she cried, "but the family's falling apart."

Across the room, Betsey started crying, too. I'd about had it with tears; they always seemed to wash away what needed to be said. Then the door crashed open and I flinched in Momma's arms as Wilma rushed inside. "Momma!" she cried, panic in her voice. "Momma, somebody's out there!"

"What?" Momma said releasing me.

"Somebody's out there. There's a fire burning up toward the Trimbles." Wilma was pale and shaking. "What'll we do?"

"Thought you women could handle things," I challenged. "So take care of it, Wilma." I pointed to my carbine against the wall. "Take it and go see for yourself."

"Momma," she begged, "please tell me what we need to do."

"Maybe one of us should stand watch," Momma said wringing her hands.

"What good'll that do?" I said to Wilma, not

Momma. "You women thinking you're so good, you wouldn't shoot if you had to."

"We'd wake you," Wilma said.

"I'm going to bed," I told them and stepped toward the door, Wilma grabbing my arm as I passed.

"Please don't do this to us, please, Clem," she begged.

Then I cocked my head at her and gave her a hard look and a mocking smile. "I already scouted it out, the fire." I grabbed my carbine.

"And?"

I paused. "It's our guardian angel. Any night you see that fire, you can sleep at peace, but if you don't see it, then you best worry for your life."

Wilma's hand went to her throat.

"Now I'm going to bed."

Taking my carbine, I stepped out the door into the dogtrot and climbed the ladder into the loft, knowing the girls were still fretting over the fire and angering over me. But I'd put up with enough of their weak-kneed worry.

I was still awake a couple hours later when they finally tired and went to their own beds. Only then could I manage some sleep, dreaming of Mary Lou Russell. Always, she disappeared into the darkness as she had at Dunker Bend.

Come morning, I was the first one up, and I got the stove going and a pot of coffee boiling. As I stepped outside to the woodpile to replenish the woodbox, I thought I glimpsed Nathan by Vernon's grave. When I returned he was gone, and Momma was in the kitchen waiting for me. She was as somber as an undertaker.

"We've a full crop in the field to pick and just three of us to do it," she said.

I counted four of us. "You're leaving Betsey out."

Momma shook her head. "No, *you*! We can't use you. You might get shot. Just us women'll pick cotton. It'll take time, but we need the crop to pay our debts. You'll stay inside during the day."

I lifted my hand to protest. It wasn't that I wanted to pick cotton, because I hated it, but my pride was wounded that I was being protected so.

"You're a Barton and in danger."

"I'm not scared," I answered.

"Men never are," Momma said, "but their women are. I've lost enough sons already in Vernon and Nathan and I don't want to lose another."

I never picked cotton again. I'd always vowed to quit, but I never imagined it would happen so soon. But quickly the boredom of doing nothing began to weigh on me while Momma and the girls were out in the field. Momma wanted me to stick close to the house and out of sight. Mostly, I did what she said. When Momma announced one night after supper that she was going to town the next day to buy supplies, I gladdened at the prospect of getting away, but Momma quickly informed me I was staying home to avoid trouble.

Early the next morning, I hooked up the mules to the wagon and put Momma and the girls on the road so they would pass the Trimble place before light. The day was long and, out of boredom, I hauled water from the river to the water barrel and tried a little fishing, but nothing was biting and the day seemed to pass as slowly as the scattered clouds overhead. Come evening, I was as edgy as a young bull at steering time. Just about dark I heard the wagon rattling in. I strolled outside as the girls pulled up to the porch.

"Any trouble?"

"Yes," Betsey answered nervously.

"No, not really," Momma corrected. "Let's unload, then we'll talk."

"Betsey," I said, "if you'll fetch a lamp, I'll unload your share. Yours, too, Wilma."

Wilma watched wordlessly, but Betsey disappeared inside, then shortly reappeared with the lamp. I climbed in back and tugged at a fifty-pound sack of potatoes. As I picked it up, several potatoes fell out.

"By jehu," I said, "the gunnysack's ripped."

"Watch your language, Clem," Momma scolded, picking up the potatoes. "We caught Snakey Trimble trying to steal a handful of potatoes when we came out of the store. Wilma shooed him away, but he went and got some of his brothers and they hurrahed us until we were out of town."

I grabbed the sack by the neck and carried it into the house. "They ought to leave our women folk alone." I returned to the wagon for another load, Momma right behind me.

"Feelings are running high against us Bartons," Momma said. "Most folks, including the storekeeper, figure Pa and the boys killed the sheriff. It looks like the deputy's gonna pull through, but he didn't see who did the shooting. I know this, Clem, you best not ride into Palo Pinto for many weeks. There's some talk, too, of sending for the Texas Rangers."

After I finished unloading things, I took the team out to the barn, unhitched the mules, fed, and watered them pretty good, all the time wondering where Pa and my brothers were. They were just ordinary folk, to my way of thinking, and wouldn't stand a chance against fighting men like the Rangers.

When I was done, I went back to the house, glad to see Nathan's fire burning out beyond the trees. Momma was still fretting in the kitchen.

"Maybe we should've stayed in Arkansas and none of this would be happening," she said. "I just pray the trouble's over with the Trimbles."

Momma's prayers went unanswered. When the Trimbles did strike, it was so evil what they did that it turns my stomach to this day to think about it.

The next night, Momma had sent Betsey in early from the field to fix supper. I was sitting outside on the dogtrot, watching the sun sink behind the trees and listening to Betsey humming some gospel song I didn't recognize. She was happy to be in from the field and cooking. Unlike Wilma, Betsey had a woman's outlook, accepting men for what they were and not wanting to change them as much as make one of them her own. She'd blossomed into a pretty young lady and would've made a fine wife and mother, had she lived.

I was just whiling away the time until supper and Betsey was inside the kitchen throwing together our meal. I could hear the pots and pans banging against the stove, and Betsey just kept on singing. It was so tranquil, I was getting drowsy.

And then a shrill scream jolted me. I jumped from my chair with a start and grabbed my pistol.

Betsey screamed again, and my spine crawled with fear. I'd never heard such a terrifying noise. I sprang for the kitchen and burst through the door to find Betsey sprawled on the floor, potatoes scattered at her feet. Betsey's eyes were wide with terror, and it didn't make sense, such a commotion over tripping and spilling the potatoes. Then, at her feet, I saw the cause of her terror.

A coiled snake.

My first impulse was to laugh, because I didn't hear the buzz of a rattle and figured Betsey had had a terrible fright and nothing more. Then I realized the diamond markings on the snake's back were danger signs and, though the snake was not buzzing, its tail was quivering. It was a rattlesnake!

I grabbed Betsey's outstretched arm with my free hand and pulled her away from the snake, then I aimed my pistol and squeezed the trigger. The room exploded with the shot, and the snake convulsed in death.

"Betsey?" I shouted kneeling by her and lifting her head.

She moaned. "I'm gonna die."

"Don't say that!" I screamed as Momma and Wilma scrambled into the kitchen. It was hard to hear Betsey's soft voice over their gasping cries.

"What happened?" I asked.

She looked to me, not to Momma or Wilma, but to me, and I noticed a trickle of blood from her neck and on her arm.

"I was getting potatoes," she whispered. "When I opened the sack, it struck me here." She rubbed her neck. "It bit my arm and maybe my leg when I fell."

I moved her hand from her neck and cringed at the fang marks just where the neck and shoulder came together. Then I saw the puncture marks on her right arm and her right calf as well. I closed my eyes to keep from crying.

By then Momma was sobbing. "Oh, my precious baby," she cried, "why has this happened to you?"

Wilma found the broom and brushed the snake outside. Then I heard the sound of metal hitting the hard-packed ground. Wilma had gotten a hoe and was chopping the snake into a thousand pieces. I didn't have time to think about why the snake had lost its rattle. I just knew I had to get a doctor and get one fast.

"Tie up her arm and leg to keep the poison from getting to her heart. I'm riding for the doctor in Palo Pinto."

Momma nodded numbly, then realized what I had said. "No, feelings are high against you in Palo Pinto."

I didn't stop to argue, just ran out the door to the barn. I still had my revolver, but I left the carbine, not wanting the extra weight on the ride. I saddled up quick and in minutes was galloping along the road toward Palo Pinto and the doctor.

It was the first of many hard rides I'd make over the next several months. As I rode, I had a lot of time to wonder how that rattlesnake had lost its rattle and gotten into the potato sack. It just didn't seem normal. Everything had gone wrong since Vernon's trouble with Baird Trimble.

And then it hit me with a start. That snake hadn't crawled in there. It had been put there. Momma had mentioned Snakey Trimble messing with the wagon. He wasn't stealing potatoes, but putting a snake with a clipped rattle among them. Damn the Trimbles. It was all I could do to keep from turning around and charging back toward the Trimble place.

But Betsey was back home dying, and I had a more important task than revenge, for the moment at least.

I reached Palo Pinto well after dark and found the doctor's home. Emotions in town were still keyed up, and he was wide-eyed when he opened the door to find me. I begged him to come, but he toed at the floor, stalling for an excuse. I was so exasperated I did a foolish thing. I jerked my revolver. With my pistol pointed at his nose, all of a sudden I became awfully persuasive, and the doctor agreed he could go after all. Considering the reputation the Bartons had developed since the killing of the sheriff, I guess he figured he was almost dead, too, but I had run out of alternatives.

The threat and all the trouble I'd gone to did little good except start a bad reputation I could never outlive. I got the doctor there, but Betsey's leg was all swollen and purplish. Her arm was stiff from swelling and her neck was bloated with the poison.

After giving her some medicine, the doctor studied her wounds and shook his head. "Some folks pull out of snake bites, but I've never seen one like this. If she makes it through the night, she might survive, but she'll be a cripple with a lame arm if she lives."

I felt the anger boiling in me at Snakey Trimble as the doctor gave us the news. Without thinking, I brushed my hand against my revolver butt, itching to get even, but the doctor misread me, his eyes widening to the size of dishpans.

Holding his palm toward me, the doctor defended his actions. "No, no, I tried my best."

He scampered out of the room like a scolded dog. I didn't think that much of it, but later word was that I'd threatened him just to get him out to our place and had threatened him for not saving Betsey.

Betsey lived through the night as much on our prayers as anything else, but come sundown the next day, she was delirious. Her crazed rantings kept us up through the night. Just as the first tint of dawn was erasing the darkness, she gave a final gasp and was quiet forever.

Through the wailing and sobbing of Momma and Wilma, I vowed to kill Snakey Trimble.

I'd followed a plow some and wiggled my toes in the cool of freshly turned dirt, but you don't get to know the earth until you've dug a grave. I dug Betsey's grave myself, just down from Vernon's, and it took me half a day. Inch by inch I fought the hard, layered earth.

But there were fewer layers of dirt in that grave than there were layers of hate in me for the Trimbles. They'd hanged my oldest brother and then killed my youngest sister. Both would rest side by side through eternity and there was nothing I could do. Except dig Betsey's grave.

Word had gotten out about Betsey's death, and a few folks, who left their fields, showed up come burying time. Feelings were running high against us Bartons since the sheriff's killing, and the Trimbles, I later learned, had told folks anyone who attended would be considered an enemy.

We put Betsey to rest the morning of the second day after she died. We had no coffin, so we wrapped her in a quilt Momma had made for a wedding Betsey would never have. You don't know what it does to a man to see his sister so young and yet so cold and stiff. I watched Momma comb Betsey's hair and tie her favorite blue ribbon among the curls, then straighten the lace trim on Betsey's Sunday meeting dress. As we finished, Momma kissed her bare cheek and then pulled the quilt over her head.

Wilma escorted Momma outside, and a couple men I hardly knew helped me carry Betsey to her grave. We lowered her in the ground as gently as we could and then took our places around her. Though Momma had sent for the preacher, he never showed up, and, without Stig Russell around—the Russells didn't hear about it until after Betsey was buried—there was no one to say pretty words over Betsey.

I felt miserable about that, a lump in my throat keeping me from saying anything, much less the words she deserved. Then Momma, through her tears, began to hum "Beautiful River." I was a little foggy in the mind then, my eyes fixed upon the shovel in the mound of dirt I'd piled up around the grave. It was one thing to dig a grave and another to shovel that same dirt back in over your sister. My knees turned gimpy and my head was dizzy.

Then somebody said amen. It was over, and I seemed to have missed it all. Except for the shovel. Except for covering her.

I remember stumbling around the grave and taking the shovel, then pushing it into the loose dirt and holding it over the grave until I realized that a portion of the quilt had fallen away from Betsey's face where I was about to empty the shovel. She stared at me through closed eyelids. I went weak and would've fallen in with her had not a pair of strong hands grabbed my shoulders.

"I'll handle this," said a husky voice I didn't recognize.

And I let him. My stomach churned and my head pounded. I wandered away, lost in thought. I don't know how long I was gone, but when I returned the grave was mounded over with a simple wooden cross at its head. Everybody was gone except Wilma, standing on the porch.

She strode out toward me, her jaw set for an argument. "Momma can't take any more, Clem. You men've gotta quit this killing," she said. "Let it end here, Clem, don't go off for revenge and get yourself killed."

I didn't say a thing, but Wilma could read my mind.

"We don't know for sure it was Snakey Trimble."

Doubling up my fist, I shook it at her nose. "You ever heard of a rattlesnake with no rattle? Somebody clipped that rattle, and the only person around that won't shoot a rattler on sight is Snakey Trimble. You saw him fooling at the wagon."

"Let it stop here, Clem, please! If it would do any good, I'd get on my knees and beg you to quit, Clem. Please!"

I lowered my fist, feeling sorry for her. "She was your sister, too. Don't you care about that? If I don't do it, Pa and the boys will when they learn about it."

"Listen to me, Clem. You'll only get killed. I helped bring you and Betsey into the world when Momma birthed you. Don't let this destroy any more of the lives she carried," she pleaded. "Vernon's dead. Now Betsey. And Nathan, he just as well be dead. That's enough."

Turning, I walked away, knowing she was right. Wilma always saw things as they should be and not as they were. I always figured the way things were was the way they should be, and I was festering with hate. Wilma wanted the killing to end, period. I wanted to end it with a Trimble life—Snakey's life.

I went out to the barn and waited there, just thinking. I ignored Wilma's call to eat come noon and would've stayed there until dark had I not heard a wagon approaching. Checking the load in Vernon's revolver, I saw a top-heavy wagon come into sight, and it jarred something in my memory, but not enough to knock it loose until I saw the sign on the wagon side: T. A. Adams, Photographer, Weatherford. Then I recognized the photographer from Dunker Bend. The last time we had seen him was the day our troubles began. Starting for the house, I reached it about the same time he did.

"Afternoon!" he called drawing back on the wagon reins, then setting the handbrake.

I nodded. "You came to the wrong place for any business."

He climbed down from his wagon, hitting the ground and stamping his boots on the earth. "I know it's a bad day to be calling, your sister and all, but I thought I might bring you some solace over your losses."

I felt my fists clench. Mock sympathy galled me, and I took a step toward him, figuring I'd show him not to come around to sell us something while we were in mourning, but Momma emerged from the house. Before the photographer ever realized my anger, Momma stepped between us, dabbing at the corner of her reddened eyes with the same apron she'd worn to Betsey's burial.

T. A. Adams took off his derby and smiled, watching Momma with squinty eyes I didn't trust. "Afternoon, Mrs. Barton. Let me first offer you my sincerest condolences on the loss of your daughter. You have had a bad month."

Momma nodded, and I simmered, just waiting for him to try to make his pitch.

"Some folks up the trail suggested I not come over to your place, saying it was dangerous," he paused, letting the last word hang in the air.

"I'm glad you came," Momma answered, and I knew she would give in to anything he offered to sell.

"But I wanted to present you with the tintype I took at the social. It will ease the burden of your losses no more than the weight of a feather, but perhaps it will give you a remembrance of a day when your family was whole." Adams pulled a tintype from his wagon seat and offered it to Momma.

She grasped the tintype, drew it to her breast, and closed her eyes as if she were afraid to look at it. "How much do we owe you, Mr. Adams?"

Adams straightened his coat. "Not a thing, ma'am. It's so little a loss to me compared to yours that I want you to have it free."

I was shamed for my suspicions and felt I ought to crawl in a hole, but a hole reminded me too much of a grave, a grave too much of dying, and I wasn't ready to die, not with so many Trimbles still walking around. Then I realized I had changed. Until the fight at Dunker Bend, I hadn't been so suspicious of people. After that, though, I questioned them all, and I would the rest of my life. I came to learn that if you expected the worst out of people you'd seldom be disappointed.

Momma thanked Adams and invited him to stay

for supper and the night if he liked, but he said he had other folks to visit before heading back to Weatherford. He wished us well and climbed back in his wagon. Taking the reins, he paused after releasing the hand-brake and shoved his hand inside his coat.

"I almost forgot," he apologized. "I've a letter here for a Clements Barton."

Momma nodded and pointed at me.

"On the way down, I stopped by Stig Russell's and his girl asked me to give this to you," Adams told me.

Taking the letter, I nodded my appreciation and slipped it in my pocket, not wanting to appear too eager to read it in front of Momma. Adams offered his condolences a final time and whistled at his worn horse, the wagon easing forward and making a circle in front of the house before heading back up the dusty trail.

"It's a good likeness," I heard Momma say to Wilma handing her the tintype. "We made a good-looking family." Her voice broke, and she retreated with her grief into the house.

Wilma studied the tintype, and, with a gaze brimming with bitterness, held it up for me to see, but not touch. "See what you stubborn men have destroyed?" She spun around on her heels and left me alone.

I'd had enough of her yapping and finger-pointing. Wilma was a good woman, but got to be self-righteous after the feuding started. I went down by the river, where Mary Lou and I had walked at Vernon's burial, and there I pulled out her letter and ripped the flap open, tearing a corner of the letter.

I never was a good reader, so it took me a while to figure it out. Her handwriting was delicate as a flower's touch, and she told me how she'd wait for me until the day we could get away from all this trouble. I wandered along the river bank thinking about Mary Lou until supper time. I ate with Momma and Wilma, nobody speaking during the meal. As I was getting up from the table, Momma motioned for me to stay.

"Tomorrow Wilma and I'll work the field. We've gotta have money to live on," she announced.

"I'll help."

Momma just shook her head. "I don't want to lose any more family. You'd be an easy target in the field."

"Then I'm leaving," I answered.

A strange glimmer flashed across Momma's eyes, confusing me until she spoke. "Are you gonna marry Mary Lou? You spent a long time with her letter."

I felt my face flush with embarrassment.

"Don't be ashamed," Momma said. "If your brothers had done that, they might not be in trouble now. Will you marry her?"

I answered in a whisper. "One day, but I've got a few things to do first."

"Like kill Snakey Trimble?" Wilma blurted out.

"Dammit!" I yelled striking the table with my fists, the tin plates and utensils bouncing up. "I'm tired of all your preaching, Wilma. You're getting like the Trimbles."

"Clements Barton," Momma scolded, "that is not proper language in this house or for your sister."

"I'm sorry, Momma, but I'm leaving tomorrow no matter what you say." I got up from the table and barged outside for a few minutes, staring at the gathering night and smiling at Nathan's fire out there between us and the Trimbles. I didn't feel so bad leaving knowing that he was close by, even if he was crazed.

Exhausted, I climbed up into the loft and gathered a few belongings—a spare pair of drawers, a change of pants and shirt, my vest, and my coat. Winter would be coming soon. I got a couple blankets and rolled all this together with the boxes of ammunition I had. After leaning my carbine against the bedroll and draping my gunbelt on it, I turned in, but didn't sleep well. And when I did sleep, I had the same dream, of Mary Lou Russell walking away from me into the darkness. I got up and dressed just as the sky was lighting up around the fringes, then carried my bedroll and weapons down the ladder.

Just as I was about to step onto the worn planks of the dogtrot, I heard a moaning noise. I froze. The noise came from under the trees, out near the graves of Vernon and Betsey.

That gave me a start. I'd never believed in ghosts, but I wasn't so sure for a moment. My eyes stared hard toward the two graves. After several seconds, I made out a kneeling figure there. It was Nathan. Then again, maybe it was a ghost, Nathan's reputation being what it was.

I stepped away from the house, carrying my belongings, and went out to console him. "Nathan," I called softly, then louder when I drew closer.

He looked up, and even in the dimness I could tell from his eyes he'd been crying. He pointed at the new cross beside Vernon's. "Who's here?"

"It's Betsey, Nathan. Snakey Trimble put a rattlesnake in some of our supplies. It killed her."

Nathan struck the wooden marker a couple times. "Yankee murderers!" He said nothing more, just stood up and walked toward the woods.

"Where you going, Nathan?" I asked and waited

for an answer that never came. I saw Nathan just once more after that.

I hauled my belongings out to the barn and saddled Vernon's bay. Once mounted, I rode out that morning without saying good-by. I should've kissed Momma farewell, but I didn't want any trouble from Wilma. I had no destination in mind, but I rode by the Trimble place, itching to see Snakey. But things looked dark and vacant, though I thought I saw the barn door open, then close real quick as I rode by. I was foolish to go by their place, but I felt the invincibility that goes along with youth starting out on its own.

I wanted to kill Snakey Trimble so bad I could taste it, by jehu, but I didn't know much about stalking a man or bushwhacking him. I didn't see much difference between that and him putting a rattlesnake in our potatoes. Problem was I didn't know where Snakey Trimble was likely to be except around the Trimble place, and I didn't figure I could surprise him there. You've gotta know someone's habits to ambush them, and I didn't know his.

I spent about ten days living off the land and camping out in a grove of trees well off the Palo Pinto road but close enough for me to recognize passing riders. The first evening after dusk, I heard a pair of galloping horses racing toward Palo Pinto and an hour later I heard a large number of horses riding back by. I didn't think much of it at the time because I was scared. That first night on my own was frightening. I didn't feel near as big a man that night as I had that morning when I left home. With time you grow accustomed to living out, but never to being on the run.

After ten days and no sign of Snakey Trimble, just the normal traffic on Palo Pinto Road, I was plenty tired, bored, and hungry. I pulled up camp, and after dark I headed for home, planning to spend the night, then head out in another direction.

The night was moonless, and it was after midnight before I reached our place. Everything was dark, and I waited in the woods and watched for Nathan's fire. But there was nothing. Only the sound of an owl somewhere. I tied my horse in the woods and slipped toward the house, listening for signs of trouble but hearing none. When I reached the porch, I called out in a soft whisper, "Momma, Momma." Then I advanced down the dogtrot and rapped on her door. "Momma, Momma."

Hearing no answer, I lifted the lever and pushed the door open. "Momma," I said closing the door.

She awoke with a start, the bed squeaking nervously. "Who is it? I've got a gun."

"It's me, Clem," I said. "I'll light a lamp."

"No, don't," she answered, the fear plain in her words. "You've gotta leave quick. The new sheriff's got a warrant for your arrest on murder."

I figured the strain of losing Vernon and Betsey had gotten her down. The new sheriff couldn't know my plans for Snakey Trimble. "I ain't done nothing, Momma, and you know I was at the Russells' when Pa and them shot the sheriff."

"Don't lie to me, Clem. I brought you up right and I'll not turn against you."

"But I didn't kill anybody, Momma!"

I heard Momma catch her breath and I could just make out her form moving in the bed. "What about Jessie Trimble? Did you shoot her?"

"Tooter's sister? Shot?" I couldn't believe it.

"The morning you left, she and her brother Zach

were ambushed on their place. Zach's gonna live, but Jessie died that night," Momma said. "The Trimbles saw you ride by their place that morning. They told the sheriff and he's looking for you."

"Honest, Momma, I didn't kill her." I had wanted to kill a Trimble, Snakey Trimble especially, but no girl.

"But who did?" Then Momma caught a sharp breath. "Do you think Pa and the boys came back?"

I couldn't be sure, but I thought I knew. "Did you notice a fire in the woods that night after I left?"

"No, Clem, not since you left. Wilma and I figured you'd been starting fires each night just to make us sleep better."

"It was Nathan, Momma."

"He built the fires?"

"And killed Jessie Trimble, I'm sure, to avenge Betsey."

"But he didn't know about Betsey."

I cleared my throat of the lump that was riding hard there. "The morning I left, I saw him at her grave. He didn't realize what had happened. I told him, and he just walked away from me. He's bound to have done it."

Momma began to cry, an all-too-familiar sound over the last few days. "And the sheriff'll never believe it. You gotta get away, even if you didn't do it. Nothing is safe here anymore. Just leave. I filled a bag with supplies and left it on the kitchen table in case you came."

"Thanks, Momma."

Momma got up from the bed and pushed her way toward me. "Don't get yourself killed." She hugged me.

I squeezed her back. "It don't seem right, all this happening," I said. She cried more when I released her and lifted the door latch. "I'll hide out at Jumble Rocks for several days. If Pa or the boys come back, that's where they can find me." The sound of her sobs accompanied me out the door.

Quickly, I slipped into the kitchen, grabbed the bag, and smiled at its weight. Momma had packed plenty of supplies. Heading back outside, I worked my way slowly back to my horse, stopping now and then to listen. All I heard was the same owl complaining of the cool night breeze. I found Vernon's bay grazing. I'd taken to calling him Pal because he had been my only companion for the past ten days.

I rode Pal away toward Jumble Rocks, one of roughest spots around the Brazos River. At one sharp crook in the river, flood waters had disgorged huge boulders on the south bank. The soil was rocky and poor there and wasn't worth a damn for anything. Also, Jumble Rocks was off even the minor trails and had a bad reputation. Some folks said it was haunted by an old Comanche who'd had his head blowed off by Rangers. Others said it was crawling with rattlesnakes. I didn't much believe the Comanche tale. And, bad though they were, snakes didn't shoot like the Trimbles and the law.

For several days, I laid low there in Jumble Rocks, never seeing another person. Being on the dodge is about as bad as being in prison. I didn't mind the loneliness because I was never much around folks, but the boredom was hard. The days were growing shorter and the nights were becoming colder and the ground was just hard. During the day I gathered firewood, watched the clouds, killed the rattlesnakes I came across, snared me a cottontail when I could, took Pal out to graze on what grass I could find, and watched the north for the approach of bad weather and the south for the approach of people.

Then, after a week or so—I'd lost count of the days by then—I saw a rider approaching from down river. I grabbed my carbine and scampered among the rocks to check that Pal was hidden and well hobbled. Satisfied he wasn't going anywhere, I climbed up among the high rocks for position. Then I waited.

And the rider headed straight for me!

My nerves tingled like ice water. Then I recognized the rider and the ice melted from the heat of my rage.

It was Snakey Trimble, by jehu!

Had he come looking for me? He couldn't know! He was riding in too casual for that. I'd surprise the son of a bitch like he'd surprised Betsey.

I realized I was holding my breath when Snakey pulled up on his horse not thirty yards away and dismounted, never once looking up, but always watching the ground. He tied his horse to a mesquite tree that had squeezed out of the soil between two rocks. Then Snakey pulled an empty gunnysack from under a saddle strap. I let out my breath slow and took a steady aim on his spine, just beneath the shoulder blades. I held my breath again as my finger tightened on the trigger. Then Snakey bent over and picked up a long, straight tree branch. He started a strange ritual, and I held off firing because I was puzzled. Snakey worked his way among the rocks, disappearing from sight for a minute or two, then reappearing. At first I couldn't figure it out, and, even when I realized his sack had something in it when he came back into sight, I would've never guessed the contents. In a clearing just beneath me, he bent down on hands and knees and jabbed his long stick beneath the rocks, shaking it hard and then dragging it out.

Then I heard a buzzing, and my stomach churned.

He swatted with the long branch again and stood up quick as a rattlesnake the length of my arm slithered out of the shadows of the rock. Then, with a vee at the end of the branch, he pinned the snake to the ground and bent over, slipping his hand along the snake's writhing body until he pinched its head between his thumb and fingers. The branch fell away and Snakey slowly stood up, talking to that snake and laughing just enough to make it hard for me to understand what he was saying. He retrieved the gunnysack with his free hand and lifted it to his lips, where he bit at the cord that was tied around the top.

That was when I plugged him.

I aimed carefully, not going for the spine this time, but for the shoulder, to wound him. I held my breath. Then I squeezed the trigger and Snakey's mumbling was shattered by the explosion of my carbine.

Snakey screamed and tumbled forward, tripping over the stick at his feet, the rattler falling free and hitting the ground in a deadly coil by Snakey's thrashing body. The rattler struck once, twice, three times on the leg before Snakey rolled out of range.

Even from my perch, I could see the terror in Snakey's eyes and relished it so much I did a foolish thing. I stood up so Snakey would know who killed him. "You son of a bitch," I yelled, "this is for Betsey!" I lifted my carbine to my shoulder, sighting on his heart just as he jerked his revolver from his holster. My carbine roared again, and the thud of the bullet told me Snakey was a dead man.

After waiting a while to make sure no one had followed Snakey or heard the gunfire, I worked my way down to his body. He was sprawled there, his vacant eyes staring toward the cloudless sky, his innards soaking the soil. Death is a humbling experience, even in the presence of an enemy. I found it hard to stare at him long, but I had no trouble spitting in his face for what he'd done to Betsey.

Though my stomach was against it, I searched his pockets, finding ten dollars in coins and a small pistol he carried in addition to his revolver. I guess that made me a robber in the eyes of the law, but Snakey had no use for them so I slipped the money and the pistol in my own pocket. I pulled his revolver from his cold hand and tossed it among the rocks. Going to his horse, I took his carbine, busted the stock against a rock, and threw it away, satisfied that those weapons wouldn't turn up on a Trimble again. Searching his saddlebags, I found a box of shells for the small pistol I'd pocketed.

Then I worked my way back to my camping spot, gathered my belongings and what foodstuff I had left, and carried them down to where Pal was grazing to tie them atop the bay. Returning to my camping spot to hide any sign people might find that would link me to the killing, I passed Snakey's nervous roan.

Tempted to steal Snakey's horse, I held off against that. The law had less mercy for taking a man's horse than his life. I wanted the county to know Snakey was dead, but doubted folks would find him unless I helped them along. So, I grabbed Snakey by the hands and dragged him over to his horse, which was as skittish as me. I struggled against Snakey's weight, but somehow managed to work him up and over the saddle on his nervous horse, stamping and blowing at the smell of blood and shaking his head so much that I feared Snakey would fall off before I could tie him down. I slipped my hand in his saddlebag and pulled out a length of rope he used to stake his horse. I tied the rope around his feet and slipped it through the stirrups and tightened it over his wrists.

Just as I was about to untie his horse, I noticed the gunnysack full of rattlesnakes. I considered leaving them, but I realized how much Snakey would've loved them. Though it sent cold shivers up my spine, I picked up the sack and untied the twine around its neck, then carried it to Snakey. Stretching my arms out, I opened the top of the sack just enough to slip it over Snakey's head. Then I let out the breath I'd been holding and tied the sack around his neck with the twine.

That was a dumb thing to do because it turned even more people against us Bartons when Snakey was found, his head bitten and bloated. Folks didn't know for sure, but they blamed me just like they'd accused me of killing Jessie Trimble.

Untying Snakey's roan, I slapped him on the rump and he darted away, terrified by the load. Once in the clear, the roan galloped toward home. I gave the roan a few minutes, then returned to Pal and rode out with no particular destination in mind, but home in my heart. Over the next three weeks, I made a circle, heading over into the neighboring counties, then swinging around Palo Pinto.

The weather had turned cold and the wind taunted me about the even colder days ahead. Being on the dodge is bad enough in the spring and summer, but in the winter it's every shade of misery. You need a fire for heat and meals, but fires attract attention, the last thing you want. In that type of weather, only a fool or a man on the dodge would be out. When a norther blows through, the chill cuts to the bone. When it sleets and snows, every breath aches and every joint turns muddy, then stiffens on you.

During those three weeks of wandering, I camped out every night in a different place, every night with only the winter clouds or icy stars for a roof. I pined for Mary Lou Russell, but all I'd touched had turned to trouble, and I feared if I visited her I'd only spread the misery her way. I got so lonely I headed for home despite the danger and arrived mid-afternoon.

I approached through the trees, tied Pal, and eased my way to the edge of the clearing. First I saw the barn had been burned and then I spotted Momma working alone in the field. I wondered where Wilma was as I emerged from the trees and marched into the cotton stalks, thinking Momma would hear me, but she just kept on working, never looking up from the stalks, now black and stiff, the bolls leaking their cotton. More than three-quarters of the field remained to be picked. I knew Momma would pick it until the last wad of cotton was cleaned out. Or until she died.

Drawing nearer, I called out, "Momma!"

She flinched and spun around with her hand to her mouth. Then her hand fell away to expose a smile lined with sadness. She dropped her cotton sack and ran to me with open arms. "Clem, you're home."

I grabbed her, and she buried her head into my chest.

"You can't stay, Clem. The law's looking for you. They think you killed Snakey Trimble."

I didn't answer.

"Somebody shot Snakey and then tied his head in a gunnysack filled with rattlers," she said. "How can people do such?"

When I didn't answer again, I felt her body go stiff, and she lifted her head from my shoulder.

"Oh," she said, and I knew she'd figured it out.

"Where's Wilma?" I asked, not that I particularly wanted to see her, just that I felt easier changing topics.

Now Momma didn't answer for a moment. When she did there was resignation in her voice, and she broke out of my hold. "Wilma's left for good. She and Pa had a fight."

"Pa? He's home?"

Momma shook her head. "He rode in one night to check on us and rode out the next morning. In between, he and Wilma got into a fight. She's just like him, stubborn as a mule."

"Let's get in the house," I said, uneasy at standing in an open field that close to the Trimbles.

"Your horse?" she asked.

"He'll graze fine out in the trees." We walked toward the house.

"Wilma accused Pa of destroying our family and Pa said he was glad none of his boys had Wilma's yellow streak in them or he'd be shamed to death. Bartons were gonna watch out for Bartons, he said. Wilma stared at him with those cold eyes and answered that we were becoming murderers just like the Trimbles."

Momma trembled as we reached the house, then she stopped on the porch. "Then," she started and couldn't finish without dabbing at her eye with her sleeve. "Then Pa slapped her hard, knocking her to the floor. She never whimpered or cried out, just stared at Pa, shaking her head. There were tears in her eyes, but I don't know if they were from her pain or her shame. She got up slowly and left the room."

I took Momma's arm, leading her to a chair in the kitchen.

Leaning forward and propping her head in her hands, Momma sobbed a minute. "I'm sorry, it's just everything's going bad for us." She caught her composure. "I told Pa he was wrong and he told me to shut up. About an hour later, Wilma came back in while I was putting supper on the table. She was in her coat and she was carrying a bag of belongings. "I'm going away, Momma. I won't be back," she said, then kissed me.

"You'll be back, you coward," Pa said, but Wilma never looked his way. Even though it was getting near night and a blue wind was blowing in, she walked out. And she won't be back, Clem, cause she's as stubborn as Pa and he'll never apologize."

"It'll get better," I lied.

"No, it won't, Clem. Too much's gone bad. Best thing that could happen to me now would be for you to marry that Russell girl and leave Texas. Start fresh somewhere."

I nodded, feeling the twin pull of both family loyalty and of Mary Lou Russell. "I will when the time comes."

"Time's running out," she said. "The new sheriff has called for the Texas Rangers to come in and put an end to this violence. And they've brought in a company of Rangers under Henry Brooks. There's been so many killings in the last two months, not just Bartons and Trimbles, either, but we're getting blamed for most all of them."

"Are we being blamed for burning our own barn, too?"

Momma flinched with terror. Her voice shook when she answered. "Somebody must've seen Pa here. He stayed the night with me and left early the next morning. That night I was alone for the first time since we'd been in Texas, nobody in the house but me. I was lying in bed, not sleeping, when I began to smell wood burning and then I saw the light of a fire flickering off the wall in my room. I went to the window and opened the shutter just enough to see the barn ablaze. Then the shutter slammed into me and the wood splintered, a couple fragments hitting my arm. That's when I heard the gunshot. I barred the window and prayed the rest of the night."

I lifted Momma's head from her hands and looked at her right arm, where a couple red slashes of flesh seemed to be healing okay, but a third was all white and festered. "You need a doctor."

She grabbed my arm. "I'll manage," she said, then released her grip. "I've a letter for you from the Russell girl. It's in my bedroom," she said getting up and leaving me alone in the kitchen.

When Momma returned, I snatched the letter from her and ripped the flap open.

"Sit down and read it," Momma said. "I'll fix you some supper. If you're like Pa, you could use a good hot meal."

I fell into the chair, pulling the letter from the envelope and holding it up to the light seeping in through the open shutter. Mary Lou said she missed me and that she loved me and that she was waiting for the day we could marry. She'd included a letter addressed to her, as if I had written it. It said I loved her and would marry her when the time was right.

Momma offered me a pencil. "I'll get you paper to reply."

"She sent me paper," I answered taking Momma's pencil and scrawling that I loved her. It was then I decided to marry her when the weather turned good and we could leave Texas. I dropped the pencil and folded the letter.

"Want me to give that to the next rider going that way?"

"No," I answered, "I'll deliver it myself." I gulped hard before I made my next admission. "I'm gonna marry her come spring and leave Palo Pinto County."

The skillet slipped from Momma's hand and fell hard against the stove. She commenced to crying. As I stood up to comfort her, she rushed to me, smothering me with her arms. "That's the only good news I've had since the social at Dunker Bend."

The aroma of bacon and creamed corn and biscuits was filling the room, and that was the best thing that had happened to me in several weeks. It was a smell I'd forgotten, being on the dodge.

Momma must've read my mind because she released me, wiped at a tear sliding down her cheek, and studied me. "You've shed some weight." She retreated to the stove, forked the sizzling bacon, and tossed it head over heels back into the splattering grease, then stirred the creamed corn. Then she placed two tin plates on the table and a knife and fork by each.

I figured I might help, so I checked the water barrel. It was empty. I reached for the rope handle of the water bucket to haul water, but, before I could pull it off the nail in the wall, Momma grabbed my arm.

"Take a seat. I can carry my own water. You stay here so I can just look at you, enjoy you a while."

The stern look in her eyes told me not to argue. And it was a good thing. By the time I had settled back in my chair, I heard a horse nickering outside.

"Hello," came a voice foreign to me.

Momma's eyes went wide, and her flesh, even over that hot stove, turned pale. "The law!" She flew from the stove to the window, reached out, and grabbed the shutters, pulling them in and barring them.

I slipped my revolver out of my holster.

"No," she whispered, her eyes wide. "I'll flush him away."

"Mrs. Barton!" the voice shouted. "I'm Texas Ranger Henry Brooks! Who's home? I'm carrying warrants for your husband and boys."

Momma took a deep breath and seemed to mouth a prayer at the kitchen door. I slipped by the window, cocking my pistol.

"You hiding anybody?" the Ranger asked. "I've got warrants for them if you are."

Momma stepped outside. "Where were you when my barn was burned down?" Momma was defiant.

I figured I might jump out the side window and make a run for Pal. I heard the saddle leather creak from the weight as the Ranger dismounted and his boots hit the hard-packed ground.

"I intend to search your place," he said.

"That's against the law!" Momma shouted, the terror rising in her voice like rushing flood waters.

Brooks laughed. "I'm the law!"

Damn, I thought, *no chance for escape*. I leveled the gun at the door, figuring I'd at least get the Ranger, though I realized I was getting into the deep waters of trouble if I killed a Texas Ranger. I heard the Ranger step up onto the porch.

"Don't!" Momma yelled. "This is my home!"

I had only one chance—the water barrel. In two strides I was at the barrel.

Momma screamed. "Get your hands off me!"

It took every ounce of restraint I had not to run outside and kill the Ranger. I lifted the lid from the barrel and hiked a leg over the lip and inside. My eyes studied the door. The handle moved. Then it stopped. I lifted my other leg inside the barrel, almost tipping it over as I did.

"I'm coming inside!" I heard the Ranger call. "And don't try anything funny! I've got the woman for a shield!"

Gritting my teeth, I sank slowly into the barrel, my right hand holding my gun, my left letting the lid down as I hid myself.

The handle on the door moved again and the door opened enough for the ranger's gun to poke its ugly black snout inside. I let the barrel lid all the way down.

I heard the door burst open and crash into the wall.

"Don't!" Momma yelled. After a moment of silence broken only by the pounding of my heart, I heard Momma speak again. "See? No one's here, now won't you leave me be?"

"You sure are jumpy, Mrs. Barton," he said, and I could hear his footfall stalking around the room.

I knew when he was opposite me because I could smell him. I figured any moment he would lift the lid and peek inside. My revolver was just waiting to plant a lead kiss on his cheek.

He walked away, evidently stopping by the stove. "You're cooking an awfully big meal for a woman alone. Why you got two plates on the table?"

"I'm hungry," she answered. Her words were hard as granite.

"You expecting company? Your menfolk, maybe?"

"I was expecting to be left alone," she answered, her voice seeming to come from the stove now. I heard the popping of the bacon grease as she flipped the slices of bacon over again. Then I made out the sound of her lifting a pot lid. "Get your hands off me," she said. The pot lid clanged shut. Oh, how I wanted to kill that Ranger.

"Come with me. I'm gonna check each room and the loft. Then we'll have supper."

From the hard fall of his footsteps, I knew they were out of the kitchen, checking the other rooms opening out onto the dogtrot. I shifted against the barrel to get all the kinks going the same way in my legs, but that's hard to do when your knees are up to your chin and your shoulders are pinched between the barrel staves. I did as much as I could, but mostly I gritted my teeth against the pain. My legs were alternating between pain and numbness and my back was tightening up on me. I wondered if I'd be able to lift my gun with a steady enough aim to defend myself if it came to that.

The door to the kitchen banged open again. "Dish me up some of that fodder," Brooks commanded, his voice as coarse as the blade of a two-bit saw.

I heard Momma drop a plate on the table, rattling the eating utensils. When she poured the coffee, the sweet aroma penetrated the barrel and my stomach began to growl, I was so hungry.

The music of the knife and fork strumming against the tin plate told me the Ranger was eating, but it seemed to take forever, and my pain was growing greater by the second. And the coffee, it smelled so good, was contributing to my misery, until the aroma was overpowered by another smell, the odor of burning bread. Momma had let the biscuits burn, something she never did.

"Something's afire," Brooks said.

"Oh, my," Momma answered, but there was no more concern in her voice than water in the barrel that was hiding me.

I heard the stove door creak open on its hot hinges as Momma pulled the biscuit pan out and dropped it on the table.

"No wonder all your menfolk left; you serve 'em biscuits like that," Brooks said.

The stove door clanged shut, then I heard Momma's voice, so hardened with spite that it sent a shiver down my spine.

"You come in here uninvited, search my house, eat my food, and insult me. You get up and get out of here—now!"

Brooks laughed. "You gonna throw me out, are you?"

"No," Momma answered, and I heard a skillet slide off the stove, "but unless you want a pan of hot bacon grease in your face, you best leave. You make a sudden move and you'll be blind the rest of your life. Now leave."

I heard the chair scrape against the floor and the ranger's heavy footfall. "Good day," he said, then slammed the door.

The skillet hit the stove with a clang and Momma jumped across the room. I heard her slide the bar across the door. Then she broke down crying.

I fought the immediate urge to shove away the barrel lid. When I thought I heard his horse gallop away, I pushed on the lid and it clattered to the floor. I heard Momma scream. I tried to stand, but only my head cleared the barrel rim before my muscles tightened on me, then suddenly melted away under the heat of a numbing weakness.

"Clem?" She was breathless and could say no more.

"Help me. I can't get out."

She hurried across the room, her hands at her mouth. "Oh, Clem, I thought you'd escaped out the window." She grabbed me under the shoulders and strained against my dead weight.

I released the hammer on my revolver, then grabbed the barrel rim with my free hand and shoved against it, my legs straightening against their will. Pain stabbed up and down my muscles from my ankles to my back. I balanced myself for several seconds until the feeling crept back into the legs I wasn't sure I still had. Finally, I was able to lift them over the barrel, rest on the rim for a moment, then slip down and stumble toward a chair. I reholstered my pistol.

"I burned the biscuits, Clem," was all Momma said for a minute. She walked to the stove and filled a plate with the creamed corn and with what bacon was left. "Henry Brooks had a big appetite."

"And a big mouth," I answered.

"You forget that, Clem. The law has too long a memory to tangle with." She placed the plate before me and then brought me a cup of coffee.

The food filled the hole in my stomach as the feeling returned to my legs. The hot food, even without good biscuits, boosted my spirits. I ate it without another word.

Momma hovered over me like a hen over her lone chick, filling my plate until there was nothing more to eat and keeping my coffee tin full. I pushed myself away from the table when I was done, rubbing my legs and testing them for feeling. Momma scurried about the room, filling a gunnysack with food.

"This'll get you a few miles down the road."

"It won't be this good." I pointed at my empty plate.

"Been better with good biscuits."

I snickered. "It was worth it to hear you scare the Ranger off with a skillet."

"It's good to hear laughter in this house," Momma said. "There's been so little of it lately. I miss you and your brothers, Clem. And Wilma!" Her voiced lowered to a whisper. "And Betsey and Vernon. I still have them, in a way, out under the tree. I spend a lot of time out there, talking to them. They never answer, but I know they're watching over me."

I pushed myself up from my chair before my legs took root and I was tempted to stay the day. "I best be going, Momma. I don't know when I'll be back."

"Pa said he may be back with your brothers on Christmas. He figures the law won't be looking too hard for them then."

"Maybe I'll get back, too. That would be all of us except Wilma and Nathan. Have you seen any night fires in the trees?"

"Nothing. Nathan may be gone for good. Maybe that's best for us all." Momma paused for a moment. "Was it true what you said before, about taking that letter to the Russell girl?"

I felt a blush warm my cheeks. "I meant it," I admitted.

Her lips curved up into a soft smile. "I have something for you." She unbarred the kitchen door, and I heard her retreat into her bedroom. She came back holding a leather pouch. "We've never had much money, but what we've managed to save and what Vernon had totaled up to more than a hundred dollars. I'm giving you fifty for you to use to get married and get out of Texas." She gave me fifty dollars in paper money, then kissed me and wished me luck.

With the fifty dollars Momma gave me and the ten I'd taken off Snakey Trimble, I had more money than I'd ever imagined. I was rich enough to make a start for me and Mary Lou Russell. I burned to see her and offer her my proposal so we could leave Texas. Being on the dodge, I was tired of freezing in the cold, sleeping on the ground, starving every day, and looking over my shoulder all the time. It was a damned poor way to live.

I feared word was getting around I was sweet on Mary Lou and the Trimbles might be watching her place, but I just had to see her again, despite the risks. I left home and rode south about a dozen miles to cross the Brazos. Then I made a wide circle east and north, hitting the Russell place from the opposite direction. I hobbled Pal and leaned up against a tree to nap, figuring it unsafe to approach their cabin until after dark.

The cool hit with the dusk, and I shivered until my teeth chattered. When I figured it safe, I gathered myself up, straightened my clothes as best I could, unhobbled Pal, and led him toward the house. My eyes fixed on the yellow glow coming out of the Russells' kitchen window. If they'd had a dog, they'd've known about me, but I made it almost to the house without anyone seeing me.

"Hello," I called, tying Pal to the hitching post. "Hello."

The light in the kitchen dimmed and the door cracked open, a gun barrel sliding out. "Who are you?" came the voice of Stig Russell.

"Clements Barton," I called.

"Clem!" Mary Lou's voice answered through the walls, and the door burst open. Instantly, Mary Lou was upon me, hugging me and crying and laughing all at the same time.

"I love you," I whispered in her ear.

Before she could reply, Mary Lou's momma issued a scolding command. "Get in this house, Mary Lou, before you get sicker."

"I'm so happy," she said, "I feel better already." She released me. "Come on in. Supper's on the table."

Stig Russell was propping the shotgun back in the corner when Mary Lou pulled me inside. "Evening, Mr. Russell. You too, ma'am. I didn't mean to give you a start."

"It's no matter, Clements Barton," Mary Lou said. "All that matters is that you're here and safe."

Stig Russell offered me his hand and I shook it. Mrs. Russell nodded while Mary Lou's younger sisters, eyes wide and mouths open, lined up against the opposite wall as if they'd seen a ghost.

"We were about to eat," Stig Russell said. "Please join us."

"Best offer I've had all day," I answered, staring at Mary Lou the entire time. She wasn't dressed in outside clothes, but a gown and a robe over it. She looked pale, but from the sparkle in her brown eyes, I knew she was happy.

Mrs. Russell set an extra plate on the table beside Mary Lou's. Mary Lou seated herself on the bench, and the other girls each took a place, all save the youngest, who cowered against the wall.

"What's the matter?" I asked.

"You won't kill me, will you?"

I laughed, but the laugh died in my throat when no one, not even Mary Lou, joined me. "Why no, I wouldn't harm you." I picked her up and placed her on the bench. While I took my seat, she slid as far away from me as possible.

"Bad stories are going around about you, Clem," Stig Russell said. "We'll eat, then talk—you, me, Mother, and Mary Lou."

Nodding, I felt my shoulders sink with my spirits. Not even the aroma of Mrs. Russell's hot cornbread, red beans, and hamhocks could cut through the gloom that settled over me. I helped my plate without enthusiasm and ate without enjoyment, though the food was hot and tasty. Mary Lou tried to keep a conversation up, but she soon gave up. For a sweet, Mrs. Russell offered me cane syrup on buttered cornbread, but I passed it up, fearing it would only prolong supper and the discomfort hanging in the air.

"Fine meal, Mrs. Russell," I said, excusing myself from the table. "I best go tend my horse." I grabbed my hat and went outside, figuring I'd ride on. I should have jumped on Pal and ridden away, right then, and forgotten Mary Lou and the Russells, but I lingered a minute, staring at the stars, wondering where it would all end. I shrugged, untied Pal, and had a foot in the stirrup when Mary Lou came outside, bundled in her pa's coat.

"Don't leave, Clements Barton! Please!"

I couldn't read her face, but there were tears in her words.

My foot slid out of the stirrup. "If I'm not welcome, I'll ride on, no hard feelings."

"My folks don't know what to think and my sisters are scared by the stories going around. Some say you shot Jessie Trimble. I know better than that. Others say you killed Snakey Trimble. Maybe you did, I don't care. I just want you to leave Palo Pinto County for good, and when you go, I want you to take me with you."

I retied my horse and stepped toward Mary Lou. "I came to propose to you, go somewhere new, start fresh there."

Mary Lou reached for me, and I moved into her grasp. Her cheek, wet with tears, pressed against mine. "I'll marry you. I'll go with you wherever you go."

"But, your folks?"

"They like you, Clements Barton, but they've heard all these bad stories. Please, stay." She tugged me toward the door. "I must go in. I've been sickly and this cold air isn't healthy for me." She wiped her eyes on the coat sleeve, then pulled me back inside.

Her parents were alone in the kitchen, and I could hear the girls in their bedroom playing games. Mrs. Russell was cleaning the dishes while Stig Russell eyed me. As I shut the door, he spoke, his voice strong and serious. "Did you have anything to do with the killing of Jessie Trimble?"

"Father!" Mary Lou said.

"No, sir!" I answered taking off my hat, still unsure if I was welcome despite what Mary Lou had said.

"Folks say you were seen riding around their place that day. That true?"

"I left home that morning and passed their place, but I didn't hang around. I hid out a spell, figuring it was safer in the open than at home," I answered. "When I returned home was the first I knew of Jessie Trimble."

"Then who did it?" Russell motioned to me to sit down.

I cleared my throat. "I figure Nathan did it. The morning I left, I found him crying over Betsey's grave. I told him about the snake and that I figured Snakey Trimble had done it."

Stig Russell shook his head. "Nathan's caused you Bartons a lot of hard times."

Mary Lou settled onto the bench beside me, slipping her hand in mine. "Father, Clements has asked me to marry him."

I was shocked for a moment, her boldness surprising me. I'd figured to ask Stig Russell about it later, maybe when it was just me and him, not with Mary Lou there, and certainly not with Mrs. Russell hovering over us.

"That so, Clem?" Stig Russell asked.

I nodded. "That's my intention, provided you agree."

Stig Russell stood up, slowly unfolding his lean frame and walking around the table, scratching his chin. Mary Lou leaned closer to me, her hand squeezing mine tightly.

"Nothing against you, Clem," Russell started. "It's just I don't want Mary Lou getting caught up in this nasty feuding."

"I'll leave Texas with her. I'd do it now if the weather was warm. I'm tired of the feuding. I figure to get out of Palo Pinto County for a spell, get a job, earn a little money, come back in the spring, be married, and be gone."

Russell circled the table silently one more time. "I'll agree if you leave Texas."

Mary Lou released my hand so fast that I thought she was mad at me. She shot up from the bench and flung her arms around her pa. "Thank you, Father, thank you." Then she turned to her momma's outstretched arms and they fell into one another, hugging and crying. It made me uncomfortable, all this foolish emotion, but I was glad I could marry Mary Lou Russell.

Crossing his arms across his chest, Stig Russell stared at me. "Promise you'll stay out of the county until the wedding?"

"Come Christmas I plan to visit Momma. That's the only time I'll be back." I didn't mention Pa and my brothers might return then. "Rest of the time, I'll find work down south."

Russell eyed me hard still. "You'll leave Texas for good?"

"After the wedding." I nodded.

Mary Lou and her momma broke free from one another, Mary Lou coming to me and Mrs. Russell hurrying to her husband. "We'll invite everyone for the best wedding ever," Mrs. Russell said.

"Mother, we can't tell folks about it. Feelings are running high against the Bartons. We'll keep it to ourselves."

"But a wedding should be a big celebration, not a secret," Mrs. Russell argued.

I could see the exasperation in Stig Russell's eyes.

"Oh, Mother," cried Mary Lou, "I don't care if no folks come as long as I have Clem and my family here. That's all I want. When shall we wed, Clements Barton?"

"April, I was thinking. First Saturday in April. Most folks'll be busy with spring chores. Maybe we can get out of the county unseen." I dug into my pocket, pulling out the paper money Momma had given me and the ten dollars I'd taken from Snakey Trimble. "This'll buy us a buggy and a horse and maybe a few things for yourself before we go away."

"Just a minute," Stig Russell said. "Where'd you get that kind of money? Did you steal it?"

I separated Snakey's money from Momma's bills. Sticking Snakey's back in my pocket, I studied Russell. "Most was Momma's plus a little from Vernon. Momma wants me to leave, too."

Russell nodded his okay. "As long as you didn't steal it."

Maybe I should've been insulted by Stig Russell, but I just felt so beholden to him for permitting me to marry Mary Lou that I overlooked the remark. I placed Momma's money in Mary Lou's hand and folded her fingers around it, then patted the ten stolen dollars in my pocket. I didn't feel like a thief with it, but I wanted to play straight with Stig Russell.

Mary Lou counted out the bills. "Fifty dollars! Oh, Mother, I've never had so much money." She was so happy.

The four of us talked about what I'd do after the marriage. Farming was about all I knew, but I figured opportunities abounded in New Mexico Territory and we'd go there. After a while, Stig Russell offered to put Pal in the barn, but I said I'd best do it, Pal disliking strange handlers. As I left for the barn, Russell suggested I sleep in the kitchen.

When I returned, only Mary Lou remained, and as soon as I dropped my bedroll, she greeted me with a kiss.

"I can't wait until April. I'll miss you until then, but after that I'll have you forever," she said.

"Maybe this will help you remember me." I pulled her letter from my pocket and offered her the sheet she had written for me. On it was the proposal I had scribbled.

Quickly, she read it. "Oh, you did write me." She kissed me again. "I love you, Clements Barton."

"And I feel the same for you," I said.

She stepped back and put her hands on her hips. "There you go again, afraid to say 'I love you' back!"

I smiled sheepishly. "I love you, Mary Lou Russell."

We talked a bit more, but she was weak and finally retreated to bed. In the house's warmth, I slept soundly that night, knowing that come spring she'd be beside me each night to keep me warm. It was a comforting thought, but it couldn't erase that dream of her disappearing into the darkness just beyond my reach.

Come morning, I was up first and had Pal saddled before Mrs. Russell arose to fix breakfast. The cooking was almost done when Mary Lou entered wearing her best Sunday dress of blue striped cotton ticking with little white bows at the neck and shoulders.

"I wanted to look nice before you left, Clements Barton," she said, then smiled. "So you won't change your mind."

"You're prettier than a warm sunrise on a cold morning," I said, not knowing if it really made sense. She blushed, so I thought I'd done okay.

Stig Russell came in shortly after, yawning and stretching his arms. "Morning," he said, then smiled at Mary Lou. "My, my, don't you look pretty."

Mary Lou giggled and glided across the room to hug him.

"You ready for me to get the other girls up, Mother?" Russell asked.

"No, let them sleep a little later so Clem and Mary Lou won't be bothered."

When I saw Mrs. Russell put a small bowl of eggs on the table, I realized she was letting them sleep late because there weren't enough eggs for all. Her eggs, bacon, biscuits, and hot coffee settled right well in my stomach.

Mary Lou looked so beautiful and breakfast went by so fast. When we finished eating, Stig Russell and his wife lingered in the kitchen as Mary Lou walked with me out into the morning coolness.

We held one another and kissed, the last kiss before our wedding day. "I love you, Mary Lou Russell," I whispered in her ear, then released her and stepped toward Pal. If I had stayed a moment longer, I knew I would be tempted to take her with me, and she just couldn't travel in her condition in that weather. I mounted and took off my hat. "I'll be back the first Saturday in April. Let's marry at noon."

She nodded. "I love you."

I slapped Pal on the flank with my hat and I was off. I didn't see Mary Lou again until the wedding. It all seemed so sudden, the courtship, the feud. But the courtship and betrothal seemed like they were meant to be. The feud never did. I rode from the Russell place south toward Waco. The weather was tolerably cool because the sun was out. I avoided the roads where possible and took all the time and precautions of a man on the dodge.

After a few days, I approached Waco from the east, marveling that a town could be that big. I never knew there could be so many people or buildings so tall, three and four floors high. Why, there were even shops where you could buy dishes of ice cream. I'd never heard of such. All the cotton grown in central Texas passed through Waco, so it was busy. Wagons stacked with bales of cotton always seemed to be heading in and out of town.

I figured it'd be easy to find a job, but I was sapling green about the ways of the big town. After hunting a place to room and take meals, I realized my ten dollars wouldn't last long and that I needed to save as much as I could. Stabling Pal would cost more, so I was at a loss over what to do. I spent the first two nights camped just outside town and the days walking door to door for a job. Nobody was hiring, and the ones that told me what they might pay when they were hiring weren't giving more than a dollar a day. A man couldn't provide for his own keep and save up much money at that wage.

I was about to give up when I started checking stables. I was turned down twice before I stopped at the Confederate Livery Stable and Blacksmith. The barn, the gray of well-weathered wood, had a crude Confederate battle flag painted over the front door. A slender man with a limp met me as I dismounted. He wore a shirt patched at the elbows and pants patched at the knees.

"Stable your horse?" he asked nodding his approval at Pal. "Good-looking animal."

"Need work," I answered. "You got any jobs open?"

"Maybe. What be your name?"

"Clements Barton," I answered.

He scratched his chin. "Barton, Barton. Would you be any relation to any Bartons up in Palo Pinto County by chance?"

I was stunned. My lips drew tight. "Why you ask?"

"Just curiosity. I been reading about troubles in the paper about the Barton gang up around Palo Pinto."

My face flushed with anger at folks calling us a gang.

"Bad trouble," he continued. "Sheriff and several others, including a young woman, killed up that way, the papers said, and now the governor's mad Henry Brooks and his Ranger company can't straighten it all out. Seems like one of the Bartons they were after was named Clements, like you. He's supposed to have killed a woman."

"No, sir. I said Clinton Barton," I lied. "I don't know nothing about these Bartons, though I guess if we go back all the way to Adam we're some way related."

The fellow slapped his right thigh like he meant to laugh, but he grimaced instead. "My leg still carries a ball of Yankee lead from Jenkins Ferry. It pains me when I act foolish. What was your leanings during the late War Between the States?"

"My brothers fought for the South, but it ended before I got involved."

"Then, yes, you've got a job. Dollar a day and eats for you and your mount. You'll do what I need in the day and stay here at night, handling any late business we get. I've a cot in the office you can use. You can call me Elmer. Deal, Clint?"

It sounded like a good way to save some money, and I took the job. Working on a schedule that varied, I found the work never fell into a routine and the days passed quickly toward Christmas, but never a day passed that at some time I didn't think about the Texas Rangers out there looking for me like I was an outlaw. Elmer may have been suspicious of me, but he never said much, not even the day a couple Texas Rangers wandered in looking for a man that had robbed a bank in town. I was nervous as a rat at a cat meeting, but they spoke with Elmer, ignoring me.

Elmer paid me every Friday for my work. Mostly I cleaned the stables, pitched hay to the animals, watered them, brushed them, took out rigs on delivery, and handled the late-night business, which was slow except on Friday and Saturday nights, when a lot of men visited the Reservation. That was the red light section of town, with a lot of loose women available for a price. I'd heard some interesting stories about those women and the things they could do for a man, but that didn't carry much weight with me, not with Mary Lou Russell always in the back of my mind.

Occasionally I'd venture about the town, seeing the sights and watching the commerce. All I'd really known growing up was farming, but now I knew there were a lot of work I might make a living at for me and Mary Lou.

About five days before Christmas, I told Elmer I wanted to visit home and would have to quit unless he'd let me off.

He eyed me closely. "Going back to Palo Pinto, are you?"

"Yes, sir," I answered before I realized what I'd said.

His lips curled into a smile at my admission. "I knew you'd first introduced yourself as Clements, not Clinton. You don't look like a woman killer to me."

"I didn't shoot a woman."

He nodded and smiled. "If the job's open when you return and you still want it, it's yours, Clint."

"Thanks, Elmer," I said reaching out and shaking his hand.

"Most hired help I've had has been drunkards, loafers, or bastards that spent each week's pay at the Reservation. You've been dependable."

"I promised a girl I wouldn't drink again," I said. "Come spring, when the weather's warm, I plan to marry her and leave Texas. Make a fresh start. Your pay'll help."

"I hope it works out," he said, and I could tell he meant it.

Later that day, I rode out of Waco, giving myself plenty of time to make it home. I was hoping to see Pa and my brothers, but I planned to arrive Christmas morning and leave that night, figuring there would be less chance of trouble that way. It was a sad ride for me, knowing our family would never be the same, with Vernon and Betsey dead, Nathan gone crazy, Wilma run away to who knows where, and the rest of us men wanted by the Texas Rangers.

Christmas Eve I camped out about three miles from home. The night was crisp and the stars shivered in the cold and I with them. I thought a little bit about the birth of Jesus and figured Vernon and Betsey were with Him by now and probably happy, but the more I thought about it the sadder I got, until my loneliness almost convinced me to ride on in. But I had grown too cagey on the dodge to give in to my emotions, so I just waited under my blanket and wished the night away.

I forced myself to wait an hour after good light so Pa and my brothers wouldn't mistake me for a Trimble and shoot me. Pal seemed nervous as I saddled him; his ears kept flicking northward, toward home. Of course, I didn't think much of it at the time, but after I mounted and pointed Pal toward the home place, something began to gnaw at my stomach and I knew it was more than just the lack of breakfast.

I nudged Pal with my heel and he loped forward. I bent my head into the wind. Finally, I heard a faint popping noise. I kicked Pal hard on the flank and he bolted forward, using all his strength. The popping continued. Gunfire from home? I slapped Pal's neck with the reins, then bent forward and pulled my carbine from the scabbard. Nearing the final bend in the trail toward home, I sniffed the odor of smoke. As I came within sight of our place, I saw the house afire and two bodies in front.

The damn Trimbles, fine folks that they were, had attacked us on Christmas Day.

I went crazy seeing our house ablaze and Trimbles sniping at the door to keep my people from escaping. Lifting my carbine, I screamed and rode straight for the nearest Trimble, catching him by surprise. My first shot crashed into a tree beside him. He turned and screamed. My second bullet tore into his chest, knocking him away from the tree. He staggered off balance, then the rifle slipped from his hand and his knees buckled. As he tumbled forward, I recognized Shakey Trimble.

I kicked Pal's flank and raced forward, leaning low over the saddle, scanning the trees for the next Trimble. I saw a puff of smoke and felt hot lead fly over me. I yelled and fired once, twice, three times at the tree, the third bullet striking flesh, by the sound of the scream.

By then, I heard firing behind me and feared I'd been surrounded, but it was my brothers escaping the burning house, adding their fire to mine. I kept shooting until my carbine was empty, then I pulled my pistol and circled back by the trees, firing away and screaming like a Comanche.

From behind the cover of the trees came a voice that sounded like Tooter's. "Let's get out of here."

I retreated behind Sammy and Charley, who were advancing toward the trees, shooting as they went, and reloaded my weapons. Behind me I heard Momma wailing. I twisted in the saddle to see her dragging Willard's body by the hands away from the flames and toward Pa's twisted body. Momma let go of Willard after she reached Pa. Then she pulled something from her blouse as she knelt beside Pa. In her trembling hand she held the tintype, the one belonging she had saved from the fire.

"Why? Why?" she kept muttering as she clasped the tintype to her breast with one hand. With the other she alternately stroked the cheek of her dead husband and of her son as if she could rub them back to life.

"Momma! Momma!" I yelled. "Take cover!"

"You've business to attend, Clem!" she shouted back. "Don't worry about me."

I knew what she meant and I slapped the reins against Pal's neck and dashed into the woods accompanied by the cheers of Sammy and Charley. I howled all the way to the Rockpile, but the Trimbles got away and it was foolish to go farther. Turning Pal, I headed back home for two more burials, all the time wondering where those Texas Rangers were and why they hadn't kept the Trimbles from murdering my Pa and brother.

Sammy met me at the edge of the trees. "Check our horses, Clem, down by the river."

"Look after Momma," I ordered, then nudged Pal into a lope toward Shakey Trimble's body. Though he wasn't going any place, I put another bullet in him, then heard the nicker of horses by the river. I worked my way toward the noise, finding my brothers' four horses and a black gelding I didn't recognize, all hobbled. I figured they were as good there as anywhere, so I left them and rode to check on Momma.

She was still kneeling between Pa and Willard, and the tears made ugly tracks down the smoke smudges on her face. I took off my hat. "I'm sorry, Momma. I wish I'd gotten here sooner."

"You didn't know the bastards would attack!" she shouted.

My breath hung in my throat. I'd never heard Momma say a bad word in her life until then. The fire that blazed and popped at the remains of our home couldn't have burned any hotter than the blood boiling in our veins.

"We best bury Pa and Willard and leave before the Trimbles return or the Rangers show up to protect them," I said. I rode out to where our barn had been and tied Pal to a charred post, then spent several minutes kicking through the blackened remains until I found a shovel with about a foot of handle that hadn't burned off.

I carried it to Vernon's grave and began to scoop out the dirt as quick as I could. Sammy and Charley spelled me often, so the work went fast. We didn't have time to dig fresh graves in hard ground. I was afraid Momma would figure out what we were doing, but she stayed with Pa and Willard, stroking their lifeless faces and patting their cold hands. After we hit Vernon's coffin, we carried Pa's and Willard's bodies to the common grave. Momma followed us, staring at the tintype and never realizing we'd uncovered Vernon's box.

Charley took Willard's gunbelt and boots while Sammy unbuckled Pa's gunbelt. Pa was wearing an old duster—that was all he had had for a coat—and I slipped it off of him. I wanted it in spite of the two bullet holes and smudges of blood. It'd give me a remembrance of Pa. Then we eased each body into the grave. We covered their faces with their hats.

Like me, Charley and Sammy weren't much for words, so we said our own prayers silently and began to throw dirt over them. When they were buried, we replanted the marker that Vernon now shared with his brother and pa. There wasn't much else for us to do, being as the house was about burned down to embers, with nothing to save. We had the horses and the clothes on our backs, the guns, belts, and boots off Pa and Willard. I had Pa's duster. And Momma still clung to the family tintype. That was all.

I ran out to get Pal and pointed Momma and the boys toward the horses. I led Pal by Shakey and considered throwing him in the river, but decided against it. I had a better idea. "Sammy, fetch that black gelding that's not ours," I commanded. He shrugged but obeyed. "Get me a rope," I ordered Charley.

For some reason, I seemed to take over even though both Charley and Sammy were older. I got the reputation for being the meanest of the bunch. A lot of it came from my hell-bent attack to save my family from the Trimbles. Years later, I heard that the Trimble men had said I came like a demon and shot twice as accurate. Maybe it was what I did to Shakey that made me sound so bad, but you've got to remember they'd murdered my Pa and brother and tried to wipe out the rest of my family. I tied the rope around Shakey's ankles, then I secured the rope to the saddle horn. I pointed the gelding toward the Trimble place and swatted him on the rump. He bolted for home, dragging Shakey's bouncing corpse behind him. From what I heard later, the horse was stopped a couple miles down from the Trimbles. Shakey wasn't much to look at by then.

"Sammy, did anyone see you when you rode in?" I asked.

"Not that we know of. We took our time getting here and traveled in pairs so as not to attract attention."

"We were careful, real careful, Clem," Charley offered.

"Any visitors come by, Momma?"

At first she didn't realize I had asked a question. "What?"

"Anybody come by after Pa returned?"

"Nobody. Only visitor I had for days was the preacher and he was gone before Pa and the boys arrived." Then Momma's mouth dropped open and her hand flew to cover it.

"What is it?"

"I gave him coffee in the kitchen and I had plates out at the table like I was expecting company. He asked me if family was coming for Christmas." Momma's gaze fell from us to the ground. "I said I hoped so. You don't think—" She let the question hang in the air and none of us boys cut it down.

"Momma, don't go blaming yourself," I finally managed.

Holding the tintype, she looked at it silently.

"Us boys'll be on the run; you can't come with us. I want you to go stay with the Russells," I told her. "They'll treat you okay." I dug into my pocket and gave her all the money I'd earned at the livery stable.

"Pay them for your keep and give any that's left to Mary Lou. We're getting married the first Saturday in April at the Russell place."

She smiled at me through her tears, then dabbed at her smudged cheek. "That makes me happy, Clem, the only happiness I've had in a long time."

Sammy helped her mount Pa's horse and Charley handed her the reins to Willard's mare. Momma nodded and leaned over to kiss Charley and Sammy. Then she nudged her horse toward me and kissed me. Without another word, she turned away from the home place and the graves of her family.

Us boys watched her until she was down the trail and around the bend. We talked for a few minutes and then decided on a foolish thing. We'd attack the Trimble place; give them a dose of death as well. It would've been a stupid plan, us thinking we could sneak up on the Trimbles. It wouldn't have worked except for one thing—Shakey Trimble.

We rode out behind the Rockpile, tied our horses, and slipped through the trees. The Trimble place looked deserted, though smoke was coming out the chimney. Maybe it was a trap! We started to split up and take three sides of the house when Ma Trimble drove their wagon out from behind the barn. We scrambled for good cover as she drove right at us, but she was preoccupied. She stopped the team, then backed the wagon up to the door and hopped down. As she dashed inside, we sprinted out of the trees for the house, stopping by its roughhewn side and catching our breath. The wagon team fidgeted at our presence. Ever so slowly, I lifted my head to the window, half expecting to be met by a gun muzzle. Instead, I saw Ma Trimble helping Zach Trimble from a chair at the table. He was pale and losing blood from my bullet. Here was one more Trimble as good as dead, I thought, there being no other Trimble men around. I learned later they were chasing the black gelding to retrieve Shakey's body.

Ma Trimble came out of the house with Zach Trimble leaning on her shoulder. I stepped around the corner, my pistol drawn, and was about to say something when I realized she hadn't seen me. I slipped up behind her back and lifted the gun barrel over my head, bringing it down hard against her graying mop of hair. She fell to the ground without a sound. Zack collapsed on top of her.

Sammy grabbed the team while Charley kept watch should the Trimbles be tricking us. I kicked Zach off Ma Trimble. He groaned at the pain in his shoulder and then recognized me. His eyes grew wide with terror and his mouth fell ajar.

"This is for Pa and Willard!" I squeezed the trigger three times and Zack Trimble was as dead a man as ever lived. "Throw them in the wagon, Charley," I ordered, then slipped inside the house—not to steal any of their tainted belongings, I hated them so. They'd destroyed everything we owned and I figured to even the score. I found a lamp and broke it on the floor, the coal oil spreading quickly onto the thirsty wooden planks. At the fireplace, I stuck a piece of kindling into the fire until it blazed up, then I tossed it on the floor. The flame whooshed along the coal oil stain, and the room was ablaze.

Dashing outside, I gave Charley a hand throwing Zach Trimble in the back of the wagon over Ma Trimble. The horses, smelling the smoke, stomped and tossed their heads until Sammy released the brake. The animals bolted down the road. We raced back to our mounts and were on the dodge once again.

We hid a few days at Jumble Rocks, then went to Weatherford. We talked about our fights, Charley and Sammy still mad that they had let the Trimbles ambush them on Christmas. We agreed we still had a score to settle with Old Man Trimble, Lige Trimble, and Tooter Trimble. Sammy and Charley told me they'd had a run-in with the law up in Indian Territory and had killed a deputy that thought they were bad men. It was serious, all this killing, but we were like hunted animals, with the Trimbles, the Texas Rangers, and probably federal deputies out to get us. We laid low and moved often to avoid the law.

Mostly our roaming killed time until we thought it safe to go back and run down the Trimbles. Winter was hard upon us and we suffered like I'd never suffered before. The hot blood of revenge pulsing through our veins was all that kept us warm many a night. When we returned to Palo Pinto County, we scoured the country around the Brazos, hoping to surprise the Trimbles before they surprised us. We figured they were on the prowl, too.

With time, we would've gotten them, but it didn't work out that way. We were following one of the back trails one day in the southern part of the county when we happened on a camp of a half dozen men just mounting up. The whole world seemed to come to a halt as we reined up and stared at them and they at us. For a moment, all was quiet. Then I realized those stern men were all wearing badges. It was Henry Brooks and his men.

"Texas Rangers!" I yelled and jerked Pal around. Instantly, Charley and Sammy were on my heels and we were riding for our lives. I could hear my heart beating over Pal's pounding hooves, I was so nervous. I didn't have a quarrel with the Rangers—though I considered teaching Henry Brooks a lesson for how he treated Momma—so I didn't trade shots with them. I heard Sammy and Charley firing over their shoulders. I never shot at the lawmen, figuring it would only bring more trouble, and I had plenty as it was.

"Split up!" I yelled when we rounded a twist in the road. Looking over my shoulder, I saw Charley and Sammy leave the trail together. I never saw them again. Pal scrambled through the trees, dodging bushes and rocks. I was set on making the Brazos, and swimming it if any Rangers followed me. Two did.

The air was loud with their bullets snapping through the cold air. Suddenly, the wide Brazos loomed ahead of me. Pal plowed into the water, his strong stride fighting against the powerful current. I hung on to the saddle horn and let him swim. The frigid water enveloped us. About midway across, I wondered if it wouldn't be best just to let go of that saddle horn and drown in those cold waters. Then I heard the pop of their guns and felt the splash of the water from their bullets all around me. That changed my mind, and I urged Pal on. The current carried us maybe a hundred yards downstream, where we made the opposite bank out of the Rangers' sight. Quickly, we hid in the brush and trees. I wasn't sure what I'd have done if they'd followed me, but the Rangers weren't as desperate as me, and they certainly weren't as wet and cold. I shivered and my teeth chattered as the breeze pricked my bare face like a thousand icy needles.

I needed a fire to dry out, but I feared the Rangers

might find a ford and come up after me, so I rode away. Tempted though I was to head to the Russell place, I went back to Waco. It took me five days, going by back trails, circling around approaching riders, and trying to stay warm.

Since the plunge in the Brazos, I hadn't gotten warm. By the time I reached Waco, I had the shakes all over and was fevering pretty bad. After crossing the ferry into town, I headed for Elmer's stable. Falling out of the saddle, I stumbled toward the door and slammed into it, knocking as hard as my dwindling strength allowed.

"Okay, okay!" The voice was Elmer's.

The door swung open and I tumbled forward into the warmth.

"No business with drunks," Elmer scolded, then recognized me. "Clem, err, Clint—whatever your name is. You okay?"

Last thing I remember was nodding, and then my whole world went foggy.

When the haze finally cleared two days later, I awoke to the smell of stew cooking on the stove. The room was dim and I was hungry and incredibly thirsty. Elmer must've changed and bathed me, because I was wearing a clean pair of long johns and my clothes were all washed and folded in a chair beside the cot I'd been sleeping on.

I got up from bed slowly, my knees almost buckling under me when I stood up, and dressed. I found a tin plate and dipped some stew on it. Pushing a newspaper on the table aside, I dropped the plate in its place and grabbed a spoon from the apple crate where Elmer kept his cooking goods. I shoveled the food down and it landed softly in my empty stomach.

When I was on my third plate of stew, Elmer slipped in quietly, then he realized I was up. He stepped to the lamp hanging from a rafter, and flared a match with his thumbnail. Gradually, the room filled with light until my eyes ached with the brightness. "You've been pretty sick," he said, "and the news ain't good."

"I'm not dead," I answered.

He nodded. "But your brothers are."

The stew soured in my stomach.

He pointed at the *Waco Herald* in front of me on the table. "Paper says more trouble in Palo Pinto County. Says the Texas Rangers slipped up on three members of the Barton gang."

"Barton gang?" I said. "We're not a gang, we're just trying to survive."

Elmer shrugged. "I'm just saying what the paper said. A Sammy and a Charley Barton were killed in the shoot-out with the Rangers. A third one the Rangers took to be Clements Barton—or the Palo Pinto Kid, as the newspapers are calling him—attempted a daring escape by jumping into the Brazos and disappearing downstream. Rangers believe the third outlaw drowned."

"Outlaw, damn. What about my brothers?"

"Rangers took their bodies into Palo Pinto and left them on display for a day."

I felt the tears welling up in my eyes. Wilma had disappeared and everybody else was dead except me, Momma, and Nathan.

13

Despite my troubles with the law, Elmer let me stay on at the stable because I was honest and dependable and I didn't drink or spend my money on women of low morals. When I got over my sickness, I resumed my old job at a dollar a day, saving my money except for what I spent on a new suit, shirt, tie, shoes, and carpetbag for the wedding. When I wasn't working, I oiled and cleaned my guns. That swim in the Brazos had rusted my carbine and my pistol, but the little revolver I'd taken off Snakey Trimble was worst of all. I wasted hours cleaning it, figuring it was small enough to conceal in my coat on my wedding day.

By marrying and getting out of Texas maybe I could become me again, not the Palo Pinto Kid, as some Ranger or newspaperman had branded me. I was ready to marry, but time crawled by on hands and knees. After a lifetime, spring finally came. The Sunday before the wedding, I told Elmer I was leaving. He settled up with me, giving me my due and an extra five dollars as a wedding gift. He went with me to saddle Pal, grown strong and sleek on good corn and grain, and, when I was done, he grabbed my hand and shook it vigorously.

"You be careful, son," he told me. "Get married and get out of Texas so you don't get any more burs in your tail."

"She's a fine girl, Mary Lou. You'd like her, Elmer, and you'll always be welcomed in our home."

I climbed atop Pal and rode out of Waco. The weather was grand with warmth and sunshine, and the earth was colored with the flowers of spring. Everything seemed bright and promising.

Four days out of Waco and nearing Palo Pinto County, I heard gunfire and naturally left the trail, working my way forward. Cautiously, I topped a hill and observed a running gun battle a quarter mile down a little valley. Three men were gaining on their quarry when his horse tripped and tumbled to the ground, throwing the rider free. The downed man bounced up like a ball and ran back to his thrashing horse.

With the three riders charging him, the downed man jerked his carbine from the scabbard on his convulsing mount and shot his horse in the head. The animal dropped like a sack of lead, and he fell behind it for cover. The three attackers were within twenty yards when their quarry opened fire. He fired fast, efficiently, and the front rider tumbled backward out of the saddle and never moved again once he struck the ground.

The two remaining riders bore straight for the defender as his gun went silent and he raised up, holding the carbine by the barrel as a club. The two men blasted away until they were upon him. Then their mounts jumped the dead horse, the hooves of one of the horses catching the defender's head. His whole torso flinched, then fell back as the horse stumbled, caught its balance, and charged ahead. The two riders jerked their mounts around and approached the helpless man. Sitting in their saddles over him, they peppered him with bullets. I lost count and shook my head, thinking I should've gone down to help. But I'd bought enough trouble of my own without investing in anybody else's.

After wasting their lead, one of the attackers rode off to check their downed ally and the other to catch his horse. It was too late for their partner because he had fallen too hard. Shortly, the other man returned with the horse and they draped the body over it and headed north, finally going over the hill opposite me. Once they were gone, I started down for the dead man, figuring I might take any ammunition he had.

As I neared, I didn't recognize the horse at first. It was leaner now than it had been the last time I'd seen it. Then it hit me. That was Nathan's horse. I galloped over and caught my breath. I had watched Nathan die! And had done nothing! I was sick to my stomach. I dismounted and turned the body over to be sure. Even with all the bullet holes and his face a pulp, I recognized Nathan. My stomach churned more. I figured Rangers would've taken the body to town, so the three killers had to have been Pa Trimble, Lige, and Tooter. And, I had just watched as they killed my last brother—but he'd gotten one more of them. Later, I learned it was Lige Trimble.

I didn't have a shovel, but I had a tin plate and the ground was soft from spring rains, so I scooped out a shallow place for Nathan to spend eternity. I spent a couple hours digging the hole. When it was done, I checked his pistol and his gunbelt. No bullets remained. I pulled him over to the grave and rolled him in, quickly covering him. Retrieving his carbine, I walked over to his dead horse and jerked the saddlebags free, looking for ammunition. There was none. His carbine was empty, too. Nathan had run out of luck and bullets at the same time.

What I did find in Nathan's saddlebag troubled me deeply because I couldn't figure it out—a pair of manacles and a key. I couldn't explain it, not on my own at least. Years later, when I was in prison, I got a letter from Rutherford S. Simpson, my lawyer. The envelope had a note from him saying I might be interested in the attached page torn from a Fort Worth newspaper. An article about a retiring lawman was circled in ink. I wasn't interested, by jehu, in any retiring lawman, considering all the misery they'd brought me, but there's not much else to do in prison, so I read it, even if it took a long time to finish.

The story told about the deputy my Pa and brothers had wounded when they killed the Palo Pinto County sheriff after Vernon's hanging. The old deputy talked about the night he went with the sheriff to arrest Vernon. He said they had manacled Vernon and were taking him back to Palo Pinto when a lone rider got the jump on them not far from our place. This rider took the lawmen's guns at gunpoint and forced them to remove Vernon's manacles, which he took as well. This rider wanted Vernon to escape, but Vernon argued with him, saying running away would make him look guilty. Confused, his speech awkward, this rider finally disappeared in the darkness with the manacles and the guns. It had to have been Nathan, though the lawmen didn't know that. Later, when the Trimbles jumped them, the lawmen were unarmed and helpless to prevent Vernon's lynching.

Then the deputy related how he and the sheriff had met Momma and me on the road and Momma had asked him how come Vernon had been lynched without the handcuffs if the sheriff hadn't been in on it. The sheriff gave up trying to explain, the deputy said, because he figured the truth sounded too much like a story for us to believe.

I buried Nathan not knowing that, then rode away, leaving the saddle, gear, and manacles, but carrying the burden of being the last Barton man alive.

Taking it slow the next day, I camped out beside a creek just a half day's ride from the Russell place. I bathed and shaved, washing the trail dust off, and cleansed myself of the feud. Come noon the next day, I'd be a married man, taking my new bride to New Mexico Territory.

Sleep came fitfully. I knew Mary Lou was right for me and that getting out of Texas was a blessing, but I still dreamed of Mary Lou disappearing into the darkness, just beyond my reach. Before dawn, I was up and dressed in my riding clothes and heading toward the Russell place, feeling mighty good knowing I'd be sleeping with Mary Lou at my side from now on. I was full of vinegar and I welcomed the sun as it smiled over the horizon at me.

About a half hour away from the Russell place, I stopped and hobbled Pal, then unpacked my new clothes from my new carpetbag. I took off Pa's duster and laid it on the ground to stand on as I took off my gunbelt and my riding clothes and put on my new outfit, a black broadcloth coat, matching pants, a virgin-white shirt with as stiff a collar as I ever wore, and a thin tie that I wrestled with for ten minutes. Then I pulled out my new black shoes and cursed myself as I looked at the dirty socks on my feet, a couple of my toes peeking out like squirrels looking out of knot holes. I had forgotten to buy new socks. I hoped Mary Lou wouldn't laugh, but I slipped my stiff new shoes over dirty socks. I figured I'd never looked better.

Satisfied, I pitched my riding clothes in the carpet bag, then picked up the duster and took Snakey Trimble's revolver from the pocket and put it in my coat pocket. That done, I shoved the duster and my gunbelt in the carpetbag. After tying the bag on Pal's back, I unhobbled him and climbed in the saddle. The next time I dismounted, I'd be getting married.

I came within sight of the Russell place about an hour before noon, but I stayed hidden, watching the place in case something seemed wrong. Two buggies were tied in front of the house and a table was set up under a pecan tree. The adjacent fields were freshly plowed, and smoke wafted from the chimney. Occasionally, the door would open and one of Mary Lou's sisters would run out with a dish to place on the long table. Momma emerged once, and I wondered how she'd take the news about Nathan. Finally, Stig Russell strolled out, dressed in a fine suit, and stood staring down the trail as if he figured I'd be coming on that route. All seemed so tranquil and natural I overcame my caution and nudged Pal with my knee. He moved ahead and out of the trees.

Stig Russell was still staring down the road when Momma came out of the house with another load for the table. Just as she put down what looked like a pie plate, she saw me.

"He's come!" she shouted. "He's here!" Momma ran toward me with her arms wide open, and Stig Russell turned and nodded, a satisfied smile on his face.

I pushed Pal into a lope and quickly was upon Momma, drawing back on the reins and jumping off the saddle. Tossing the reins to Stig Russell, I grabbed Momma and hugged her as she kissed my cheek.

"You're okay, you're okay," she kept repeating, her voice almost breaking each time.

Russell took Pal and tied him behind one of the buggies, then returned. "I'm glad you've come, Clem," Stig Russell said, "Mary Lou was certain you'd be here, but not the rest of us."

"I wouldn't miss my wedding, now would I?"

Stig Russell looked at me straight, his eyes narrowing, like he realized he knew something I didn't. "We knew you wouldn't if you were alive, but we weren't too sure of that."

"What?"

Momma was bawling now. "After the Rangers killed Sammy and Charley, they said you'd gone into the Brazos to escape and had drowned. We feared it was so."

Then, I remembered the Waco paper saying something about me drowning. I hugged Momma as tight as I could. "It's okay," I comforted her. "But I've bad news about Nathan."

Momma pulled herself away, the tears still rolling down her cheeks. "Nathan died a long time ago. Tell me another time, not on your wedding day. You and Mary Lou are all I have now."

The door to the house opened up and I cringed. Stepping out into the sun was the preacher. That explained the second buggy. The preacher was something I hadn't figured on. I guess we needed someone to marry us, but I wouldn't've picked him. But preachers were still scarce in those parts, even bad ones, and he'd have to do. My gaze hung on him as he came our way.

"The prodigal son returned," he said. "A ghost given up from the arms of the Brazos."

His fancy words had a way of grating on me. I released Momma and stepped toward him with a menacing stride. He stopped in his tracks. Though we were within an arm's length of each other, neither of us extended our hand.

"Clements Barton," he said, "have you come to marry Mary Lou Russell? Do you love her?"

"I figure that's between me and Mary Lou, preacher."

He smiled. "Did you by chance bring a ring?"

My face drooped. No, by jehu, I hadn't thought of that.

"Yes, he has a ring," Momma said slipping Pa's ring off her finger and placing it in my palm.

Stig Russell pulled out his pocketwatch. "A quarter till noon," he said. "Mary Lou's been ready for an hour. Let's be done with the hitching, preacher."

Momma ran inside the house and shooed Mary Lou's sisters out. Stig Russell escorted me and the preacher to the table and turned us toward the door of the house. He retreated into the house, leaving me with the preacher.

"You told the Trimbles my Pa and brothers were coming home for Christmas, didn't you?" I stared hard, and he went pale. "I'd kill you right now if you weren't about to marry us. If you ever cross me or mine again, I'll see you get a close look at hell."

I smiled at the preacher as Mary Lou's sisters lined up opposite us. Then Momma came out with Mrs. Russell and they took their places facing me.

"We're ready, Father," called Mrs. Russell.

When the door opened, Stig Russell came out, and

Mary Lou Russell stepped into view beside him. I caught my breath, she was so beautiful in her white lacy dress. In her hands she carried a bouquet of wildflowers, and pretty as they were, they could not match the beauty of her eyes, the softness of her brown hair. She came to me as soft as a dream, and her innocent smile touched me, made me wonder if I was right to be her husband, me having led a hard life, killing the folks that I had. But her smile seemed to say she wanted no other man, and I figured I should've gotten down on my knees and thanked God for sending me such a lovely woman. Stig Russell stepped to me and I just stared at Mary Lou, so glad to see her, so wanting to hold her.

The preacher said something and Stig Russell answered, "I do," then stepped back from between us.

I took her soft hand and felt it squeeze mine. As I turned to face the preacher, I heard her whisper as soft as a gentle breeze through the leaves, "I love you, Clements Barton."

The preacher opened his Bible and commenced to babbling, but I detected a nervousness in his voice. I said I do at the right time, and Mary Lou Russell's fingers tightened against my hand and I forgot about the preacher for a moment and turned to her. Her smile melted my heart and her tears rolled like little dewdrops down her cheek.

Then she said I do, and the preacher told me to slip the ring upon her finger. Momma's ring was just a band and it was old and worn, but I told myself I'd get her a new one as pretty as her. I placed the ring on her hand and the preacher pronounced us man and wife. I leaned down and kissed her full on the lips.

By then I could hear Momma and Mrs. Russell crying behind us. The preacher snapped the Bible shut, and I broke off my embrace from Mary Lou, staring at him because I knew he'd done it on purpose. As I studied him, I had a strange feeling. "We should be leaving soon," I whispered to Mary Lou.

She smiled. "We'll go after we eat. I made you a pecan pie."

As we turned around, Momma and the Russells rushed toward us. Mrs. Russell hugged Mary Lou, then me. "My first son," she said.

Stig Russell stood beside her and offered me his hand. "I finally get a son and he can't stay. I'll expect grandsons."

"Oh, Father," Mary Lou chided, "we've just married."

Then Momma took Mrs. Russell's place around my neck. "I'm so happy, Clem. Go away and stay away. Don't worry about me; I'm a survivor like you."

"Okay, Momma," I answered.

As Momma fussed over Mary Lou, all the Russell girls stepped forward, curtsied, and offered me their hands, their eyes all wide, like Mary Lou had married some outlaw.

One by one we moved toward the table as Mrs. Russell and Momma scurried back into the house to bring out the final loads of food. As they did, the preacher strode piously toward his buggy.

"Aren't you staying?" Stig Russell called after him.

The preacher turned. "I must see how work is progressing on the church."

"Thank you for coming and good luck with your church," Stig Russell called, then turned to me. "It's a good sign, this church being built at Dunker Bend. Maybe things will settle down now in the county."

The women came out carrying a steaming ham

and a bowl of potato salad. "Take your seats everyone," Mrs. Russell called, then turned to her husband as he slipped beside her at the table.

"Let's pray," he said, then paused a moment. "Dear God, we come before Thee this day to share in the joy of matrimony between a man and his wife. Bless Clem, Mary Lou, and this marriage, that they may grow to serve Thy needs. And, Dear God, give them happiness, for there has been so little in Palo Pinto County these past few months. And grant that their lives be long and fruitful. These blessings we ask of Thee, Amen!"

They were pretty words, and I thought God was more likely to listen to Stig Russell's words than the preacher's. Over the next thirty minutes I ate the best meal I'd had in months and finished with two pieces of Mary Lou's pecan pie. That made her happy.

"We best be going," I said after washing down the last bit of pie with a final cup of coffee. There was more crying as the Russell women gathered around Mary Lou, wishing her well, kissing her a final time.

Stig Russell shook my hand. "You be careful. Write us when you're settled. Our prayers will be with you."

Momma stepped up next and hugged me. "You've made me so happy, Clem. Good luck!"

I moved toward the buggy. It was an old rig, the top long ago worn out and discarded, but it had a good spring seat and room in the back for Mary Lou's trunk. I untied the carpetbag from Pal and pulled out my gunbelt, then tossed the bag beside the trunk. I buckled on the gunbelt, then jerked the carbine from Pal's saddle scabbard and propped it against the buggy seat. Out of the corner of my eye, I saw Mary Lou's youngest sister with mouth ajar and with finger pointing at the carbine.

Then I offered Mary Lou my hand. She gathered the hem of her wedding dress, took my hand, and lifted her dainty foot up onto the wagon step. I blushed, because I'd never seen her bare calf before. Noticing my embarrassment, then looking at her leg, Mary Lou giggled and climbed in the seat, and I beside her.

"We love you," Mary Lou called, "and we'll miss you. But I'll write. Good-by!"

I took up the reins and slapped them against the rump of the buggy horse, and the wagon started forward, Pal nickering behind me his displeasure at eating the dust of a lesser animal.

Mary Lou waved at her folks until we were out of sight, then turned to me. "I love you, Clements Barton," she said. "I'll miss them, but I'll love you more."

She scooted in the wagon seat as close to me as she could, then laid her head upon my left shoulder. The next few minutes were the most pleasant of my life. I had a girl that would make a fine wife and a fine mother. I was heading out of Palo Pinto County for good, and I was figuring on a new start. Life couldn't've been much more promising, considering my past. Mary Lou asked me if I liked the buggy and horse, telling me they were the best her pa could find. I said they'd do, but that didn't matter as much as her being with me. She liked that and snuggled closer, her arms wrapped around my left arm.

We must have ridden like that for a couple miles, never saying a thing, just enjoying the nearness of each other. The road was shaded in places as it made its way around the hills and toward our future. She burrowed into my side as we rode down a narrow trail pressed on both sides by an outcropping of rocks and growth of scrub oak and brush. "I never gave up on you, Clements Barton. I knew we would marry. I love you too much."

Just as I was about to answer her, I felt her flinch against my arm and sag forward. Then I heard the retort of the gun.

"Mary Lou!" I cried, grabbing her with my left arm and twisting around toward the sound of the gunshot. I saw a cloud of smoke by a dead oak, its barren limbs pointing heavenward, where God must have been deaf to Stig Russell's prayers.

The buggy horse spooked and bolted forward, and I struggled against the reins, unable at first to control the spooked horse and keep Mary Lou from falling. Finally, I jerked the animal to a stop. Behind me I heard the sound of galloping hooves and knew the assassin had run away like the coward he was. I wrapped my arm around Mary Lou and held her up. She was suddenly pale, and I felt my arm growing damp from her blood.

I slapped the reins against the rump of the horse and turned the wagon around to take her back home and send for the doctor.

"Mary Lou, I love you, please don't die," I kept repeating until my throat was hoarse. All the while, she never answered, just groaned at every jolt of the buggy.

It seemed to take forever to reach the Russell place, and when I came in view I started yelling and whistling and screaming for attention. The whole family was out in front of the house when I jerked the buggy to a halt.

"Oh, my baby!" Mrs. Russell cried.

Stig Russell was beside the wagon and instantly up in the seat, helping me remove her. "Oh, God, don't let her suffer."

As Stig Russell carried Mary Lou into the house, her sisters started wailing when they saw the back of her dress covered with blood.

I just slumped forward in the seat, placing my head in my hands and weeping. With every breath I could smell her spilled blood on my coat sleeve. From inside the house I heard all the women shrieking and, a moment later, I felt Stig Russell's hand on my shoulder.

"She's dead," he said. "Mary Lou's dead."

14

I went off behind the Russell house and cried. Mary Lou was dead. And she was so innocent of all these troubles. But who would want to kill her? Surely nobody. The assassin had been after me and missed. It all became a jumble in my mind. Mary Lou was dead and nothing I could do would ever change that. But one thing I knew, I'd put her killer in a sorry grave.

Momma came out to console me. "I'm sorry, Clem. This is the worst of all, an innocent girl like Mary Lou dying."

With a sharp gesture of my hand, I waved Momma away. I couldn't talk about it. She understood and retreated into the house.

I loved Mary Lou, and now all I had was her memory. So many things—all bad—had happened since the dance at Dunker Bend. Dunker Bend had brought me so much joy from Mary Lou, but even more heartache. So many memories about that Saturday flooded my mind—posing for the tintype, dancing with Mary Lou, skulking away after Vernon denied me his horse, watching the fight between Vernon and Baird Trimble, getting into the liquor and mischief with Tooter, and going with Tooter Trimble to shoot his single-shot rifle.

Then it struck me. I dashed from around the house toward the buggy. Grabbing my carbine from the floorboard, I called to Momma. "I'll be back!" Shoving the carbine into Pal's scabbard and untying the reins from the back of the buggy, I didn't wait for a reply. I hopped atop Pal, then I slapped my hat against his flank. He raced down the trail that had not taken me away from my Palo Pinto troubles, but rather had mired me deeper in them.

Pal's stride was strong and his pride restored after the shame of following an inferior buggy animal. He was as eager to run as I was to get to the ambush spot. Shortly, the landscape matched the terrible site burned in my brain. Pal sensed my destination and slowed without me tugging the reins. I studied the terrain, taking in every tree and every rock that could hide a man, but they seemed as harmless as the cloudless sky above me. As Pal slowed to a walk, I studied the wagon tracks and hoofprints, easily finding where the buggy horse had bolted at the shot. I followed the wheel marks until they turned in the road. Reining Pal about, I pulled up and studied the trees. The dead oak with gnarled branches pointing like accusing fingers to the sky was branded in my memory. From there, the assassin had killed Mary Lou instead of me.

I navigated Pal in that direction and dismounted, tying him to a bush surrounded by a good stand of grass. Then I made a wide circle around the assassin's den, finding the droppings where he had hidden his horse and picking up his boot prints. Following the tracks, I wound up at the tree where the spring grass had been trampled by an impatient gunman. I studied the view from the tree down the road, and saw it was a clear shot. Next, I scoured that ground inch by inch, Pal staring at me oddly as he grazed.

About ten minutes later, I found what I was looking for hidden under a clump of bluebonnets. An empty hull. My fingers slipped around the spent cartridge and I felt a shiver run up my spine from touching the brass hull that had killed Mary Lou. As I studied it, the odor of powder freshly wasted convinced me it was the fatal cartridge. It was a .38-caliber hull fired from a rifle, because the killer would not have stopped to reload a single bullet in his revolver. Most area folks used a bigger repeater, like a .45, not a .38. In fact, the only .38-caliber rifle I knew of was the single-shot Whitney Excelsior Baird Trimble had given Tooter.

At Dunker Bend, I recalled me and Tooter taking that rifle out and me outshooting him because his aim was always off. Six inches to the left. Tooter Trimble had been aiming at my heart when he pulled the trigger, but his bullet had drifted into Mary Lou Russell, sitting tight to my left. I knew that as well as I knew my name.

And I knew I had to kill Tooter Trimble.

With a heavy heart, I returned slowly to the Russell place. Why did it have to be her? Why couldn't Tooter have aimed true just once so she could've lived?

Back at the Russell place, there was great weeping, and I felt out of place as I rode up. Stig Russell sat on the porch, just staring. Leaning against the house were two shovels. I dismounted and tied Pal, realizing that our buggy was gone.

From his distant gaze, Russell seemed to read my mind. "Your momma went to tell neighbors and send someone to buy a coffin. We'll bury her tomorrow."

"I'm sorry," I said, then choked up. "The Trimbles wouldn't just let me ride away from the trouble."

Stig Russell got up slowly from his chair and let out a great sigh. "We've work to do," he said stepping toward a shovel and taking its handle carefully as if it might break, his despair as great as my anger.

I grabbed my shovel and stomped after him until he stopped. We worked in silence a long time, the only noise coming from the sound of our spades striking the earth and from the noise of Mary Lou's sisters crying as they built a fire for the washpot. Later, they came out of the house carrying Mary Lou's crimson-stained wedding dress. Seeing it, I felt a knot in my throat as big as a mountain, and I worked with a fury to finish the grave.

Stig Russell was helping me climb from the grave when Momma returned. I stood on its brink, dizzy a moment, not from the hard work, but from the sight of Mary Lou's dress on the line, the dark blood stains on the back now faint smudges. She had looked so beautiful in that dress, but that was hours ago. Now, she was dead, and my wedding suit was dirtied from her grave.

Momma came up. "I promised I'd trade the buggy to pay for a coffin, Clem. Hope that was okay."

"Yes, Momma," I said turning away. I couldn't face her.

"Word's out among the neighbors what happened. They're angered. Mary Lou was a popular young woman. A lot of folks will be here tomorrow."

"What about the Rangers?" I asked.

"I don't know," Momma answered. "They're too late to do anything."

"Except arrest Clem," Russell replied.

Momma caught her breath.

"We'll keep him away from the house in case they show up," Russell said.

"I will attend the burial," I said, "Rangers or not."

Russell walked away and Momma issued a command. "Change out of your new clothes and let me wash and iron them for you."

I fetched my carpetbag from the buggy and led Pal into the trees. After removing Snakey Trimble's pistol from my coat pocket and dropping it in the carpetbag, I changed and gave the dirties to Stig Russell, who'd followed me at a decent distance.

"Deeper in the trees there's an outcrop of rocks for cover, and a spring for drinking and bathing," he said.

Leaving Stig Russell, I found the spot, unsaddled Pal, threw down my bedroll, and waited, my mind going blank from the tragedy. Toward sunset, I bathed at the spring, washing away the dirt from the day, but not the anger. It would stay with me forever.

After dusk, I heard Stig Russell approaching. "I've your clothes." In the darkness, I could barely make out his features, but I could hear the hurt in his voice. "Supper's cooking at the house. The coffin came from Palo Pinto. I'd like you to join us for supper, and the women'd like you to help put her . . ." His voice went silent, and I was glad for the darkness. He breathed deeply a couple times. ". . . to put her in her coffin."

"Yes, sir," I said, and I couldn't speak anymore. I reached out for the clothes he carried and draped them over a boulder.

We walked back toward the Russell place, neither of us speaking, even when we stepped into the house. Mary Lou's sisters, all red-eyed and whimpering, worked on supper in the kitchen. Russell didn't acknowledge them, just strode to the back room, knocked on the door, and put his hand on my shoulder. "The women'll take care of you now." He walked away as the door cracked open.

Momma was crying, the lamplight yellowing the walls inside and the coffin just visible behind her. "Come in, Clem."

I wadded my fists at my eyes and tried to rub away the hurt. I felt Momma's hand close around my wrist and pull me inside. "I'm sorry," I said to Mrs. Russell and Momma. I clenched my jaw to keep from breaking down again.

"We know you are, Clem," Mrs. Russell said. "And you being her husband we thought you ought to . . ." Her lip quivered, and then she began to cry.

Shutting the door after I stepped inside, Momma continued for Mrs. Russell. "We thought you should see her first."

For several minutes, I stared at Mary Lou, all laid out on the bed, the tears streaming down my cheeks. She was as pretty as a plucked flower in her wedding dress. I leaned down and kissed her cold lips, one of my tears dropping onto her cheek making it seem as if she were crying. "She is so pretty," I said.

"We always thought so," Mrs. Russell answered, "and Mary Lou would've loved to know you said that."

I slid my arms under her and carried her to the coffin, gently placing her inside, my tears dripping on her clothes.

The women straightened her dress a final time, then brushed her hair, Momma clipping several locks and braiding them into a ring for me. I slipped it over my ring finger. In the dim light, she looked as beautiful as she had only hours before, when we were married. I still couldn't believe she was dead, and wouldn't believe it until the first shovel of dirt was thrown on her coffin. There was a gritty reality to that which made death, if not acceptable, at least believable.

Then there was nothing to do but wait until morning. We went into the kitchen and sat down at the table. I wasn't hungry, but I managed a little food and then escaped outside into the darkness, the image of Mary Lou's stilled body gnawing at my brain. I stumbled out to my bedroll and crawled in, hoping sleep would blot out the day's tragedy and let me escape from my regrets. But the night was long and my regrets were many, and when I slept, all I saw was Mary Lou. And then there was the sound of the wagons, arriving in a steady flow. Since dawn, the good folk of Palo Pinto County came to bury one of the best that ever lived.

I got up and saddled Pal because I'd be leaving after the burial. I took the washed and ironed suit from the boulder and changed clothes. I strapped on my gunbelt and retrieved Snakey's pistol from my carpetbag. As I slipped the pistol into my coat pocket, I fetched my carbine and kept it by me. If the Rangers came, I wouldn't be taken until Mary Lou was laid to rest proper.

Dressed and armed, I mounted my bay, worked my way within sight of the house, and waited. I'd never seen so many people for a funeral. There was as many or more as attended the social at Dunker Bend. Folks began gathering around the grave, and I saw a commotion at the house. Then the coffin was carried out and I felt weak-kneed again. I took a deep breath and nudged Pal from the cover, carrying my carbine. All eyes were on the coffin, and I got within fifty feet of the grave when I saw the one person that made my blood boil—the preacher.

Our gazes met and the hatred flared between us. Then I heard a kid yelling something I couldn't make out. When I glanced at him, he was pointing at me and creating a commotion while his momma was trying to hush him. There was fear in the eyes of the women and several men. I figured I had a reputation more dangerous than I was.

The coffin and I arrived at the grave at the same time. I took off my hat, staring at the menfolk, trying to see if any Rangers were among them. None had that cold-eyed stare that was issued with a Ranger badge. I breathed easier and guided my mount through the crowd to the coffin, waiting for the preacher. He began to spout a sermon on the mysterious ways of God and the unseen hand that guides the destinies of us all. He said no one knew why Mary Lou had to die, but that was a lie. I knew she'd died because Tooter was a miserable shot and possibly because the preacher had tipped the Trimbles off about my wedding. All around me, people were sobbing. I guess what bothered me most was that the son-of-a-bitch preacher kept calling her Mary Lou Russell, never saying that he'd married us. The insult stung because she was my wife that he was talking about and he never said a thing about me, though he mentioned the parents and sisters Mary Lou would leave behind. I figured I might kill him, too, one day. But this was not the day for that.

After the preacher said his final prayer, Stig Russell stepped forward, telling folks yesterday was the happiest day of Mary Lou's life because she'd married me. He told them we were leaving the county to get away from the troubles when some coward shot her. "Remember Clements Barton in your prayers, too," he offered staring coldly at the preacher.

Then men stepped forward and lifted the coffin up as ropes were passed under it. Then they moved the coffin over the grave and slowly let it disappear into the cold earth. Several other men stepped forward with spades and began to cover the coffin. I watched until the men mounded the grave over. Stig Russell put his hand on my arm.

I grimaced. "I'm sorry, Stig. I'd never returned if I knew she was gonna get hurt."

"She'd've been disappointed if you hadn't."

"See that you get a good stone for her." I dug into my pocket for the money Elmer had paid me. I pressed the money into his hand, keeping for myself the ten dollars I'd taken from Snakey Trimble. "I wish I hadn't brought so much trouble and sorrow to everyone."

Stig Russell nodded his understanding.

When the stream of mourners finished passing Mary Lou's grave, it was covered not just with dirt, but with wildflowers and the small pieces of broken china, shells, and colored stones the children had brought. Others had loved Mary Lou Russell, too.

I took a final look at my wife's grave, then turned my horse around. I shoved my carbine in place, thankful the Rangers hadn't arrived, and galloped away, leaving my future behind me, buried in a narrow grave with wildflower bouquets and colored glass atop it.

I didn't have any place to go. I figured Tooter'd be laying low and there was no sense in tracking him down yet. So, after a few days on the trail, I headed back toward Waco figuring I'd settle in with Elmer and earn a few dollars. But when I rode into town it was late, and I found myself passing through the Reservation. The sounds of women laughing and a jangling piano were so lively—not like all the death I'd seen in the last few months—that I nudged Pal over to a hitching post and dismounted. There were a couple saloons doing a lively business, but I was more interested in female companionship. I hitched up my gunbelt and lowered my hat, then strode up the steps of the brothel with the lively piano music. Not accustomed to these things, I knocked on the door until an older woman with heavy powder on her cheeks and thick paint on her lips opened up.

"Well, well," she said, "You don't have to knock, sonny. Just come on in and let one of my girls show you a good time, provided you've got five dollars. My name's Emma."

I nodded with dwindling enthusiasm at the thought that her girls might be as gaudy as her.

"Shut the door behind you," she commanded, then walked on ahead of me. I obeyed and followed her swaggering hips down the hall. Reaching a wide parlor entrance with strings of red glass beads hanging like a curtain before it, she held out her hand. "Five dollars and you can take your pick."

Digging into my pocket, I pulled out the ten dollars that had last belonged to Snakey. Emma grabbed the money.

"You've been saving up for tonight, haven't you?" Emma said. She tucked the money into the folds of her dress at her bosom. "You're good for two times."

I lifted my hand to protest, but hers met mine instantly with a five-dollar bill which appeared out of nowhere.

Emma smiled, the effect ruined by the random arrangement of her stained teeth. "I wouldn't cheat you." She parted the beads to the parlor as calmly as she would probably spread her thighs. "Look pretty, girls," she commanded.

Entering the parlor, I saw a black man pounding on the ivories with the same exertion it would take for a dentist to straighten Emma's teeth.

Two girls were reclining on a couch and two more were standing behind it, all smiling as if they loved me—or my five dollars. My gaze went from girl to girl, finally resting on one of the seated girls, who was holding a pillow embroidered with flowers and the words Forget Me Not. She had the softest eyes of them all, not hardened like Emma's or the other girls'. Dressed in a chemise, she held the pillow in front of her female parts.

"Want a drink while you decide?" Emma offered.

I pointed at Forget Me Not.

Emma offered a hollow laugh as reassuring as a rattlesnake's buzz. "All you young-uns go for Fay."

As I shrugged, Fay stood up and the pillow fell away. I should've felt excited seeing her in just the chemise, but I didn't. Fay grinned and reached for my hand.

"Has Ferdinand had you yet?" Emma asked.

"Nope," Fay answered dragging me away.

Emma looked at me. "You young-uns are quick, so it shouldn't matter, but Ferdinand the Bull comes in twice a year from out in the sticks and takes on all the girls. Tonight's his night, so he gets them when he wants them. You'll get special treatment, too, when you're a regular."

Fay dragged me down the hall and into the last

room on the left, shutting the door and latching it behind me. The lamp light was dim, and it helped hide the flush of embarrassment that was heating my face. Now that it was just the two of us, I didn't feel right about this, like I was betraying Mary Lou, and like somewhere she might be watching. I twisted the braid of her hair around my ring finger.

I collapsed into a chair and stared at the bed—the covers pulled back, ready for use—and I was useless. Fay stepped between me and the bed, her chemise falling down to her ankles. Her naked body swayed before me for the taking, but I couldn't do it. She stepped toward me, bent down, and patted my thigh. "You okay?" Her hand moved to my chin and lifted it up until my eyes met hers. "It's okay if you'd rather not. No one will know."

"Thanks."

Fay smiled, patted my cheek, and then retrieved her chemise. "She must be a special lady," she said wriggling into her undergarment.

I nodded and waited, Fay sensing my loneliness but not intruding upon it. The silence was broken maybe half an hour later by Emma, rapping on the door.

"Your ride's over, young-un," she called. "Get out so we can move Ferdinand in."

I stood up and stepped toward the door, but Fay grabbed my hand. "Let him get dressed," she called. "He may look like a first-timer, but he knows what he's doing." She winked at me.

Judging the timing was about right, Fay slid the latch and opened the door. I stepped outside into the hall and looked at Emma, her wide behind blocking the hall two doors down. I pulled on my hat as she opened that door and whistled inside. "Okay, Ferdinand, the next one's waiting at the end of the hall."

I made like I was straightening my clothes and adjusting my gunbelt, figuring I couldn't get down the hall anyway, not with Emma there and Ferdinand about to come charging out. From down the hall came a whoop and a holler, and a scrawny old man stumbled out into the hall wearing his drawers, his boots, and his hat, all askew, and carrying the rest of his clothes. Ferdinand mumbled something to his victim and tripped down the hall toward me.

There was something familiar about his voice. I stared hard, my hand slipping instinctively to my revolver. And then I recognized him.

Old Man Trimble! The pious old buzzard must've been trying to convert every prostitute in Waco.

Trimble came toward me, deep in thought on the sermon he'd deliver to Fay. At her door, he paused and looked up at me with a grin that died on his lips as he saw my revolver pointed at his heart.

Two blasts from my .45 ended his whorehouse preaching.

The girls took to screaming after I shot Old Man Trimble, and all I remember was chasing Emma's stampeding buttocks down the hall. The next thing I knew I was outside on Pal, galloping out of the Reservation and Waco. The piano music had died with Old Man Trimble, and behind me all I heard was women shrieking, a few men shouting, and what I took for a gunshot.

I reached the edge of town and disappeared into the darkness. If someone gave chase, they never came near me. But I had little to fear, brothel killings attracting little interest in Waco when the victim wasn't a local man. I don't think the law ever identified Old Man Trimble in Waco, and folks in Palo Pinto County figured he turned yellow or got tired of living with scrawny Ma Trimble and ran away. So, while I was proud of killing that hypocrite in a brothel, nobody ever knew it was him that got killed or me that killed him. Some times, you can't enjoy vengeance just to save your own hide.

The next several weeks remain a blur in my mind. I stayed on the move, living off game I could kill and the meals I could barter for my labor. I worked my way south all the way to San Antonio, even seeing the Alamo, or what was left of it, then headed back north, suspicious of every man I met, wondering if he was the law. I never felt like an outlaw, always figuring it was some other fellow, but the law thought differently. I never killed nobody to rob them or out of meanness, like some men of that time. The Trimbles that I killed had wronged my kin or planned to. But sometimes when you become known as an outlaw, you're no longer responsible for all the bad deeds that are blamed on you. I was said to have robbed a couple stages, killing one of the drivers, and to have bushwhacked a half dozen men to satisfy my thirst for blood. None of it was true, by jehu, none of it. I never killed anyone but a Trimble, never had a desire to, excepting the preacher, who I would've killed had things worked out.

On the dodge, I never had a moment's ease. Most times the law's not after you, but you worry that everybody knows you and your past. Of course, a past was all I had—no future once Mary Lou was dead. I saw her nightly in my dreams, disappearing into the darkness. And every morning after that dream, I'd wake up in a cold sweat and cursing Tooter Trimble for keeping Mary Lou from me. I wondered if Tooter had shot her intentionally, knowing he couldn't have hurt me more had he killed me. After a while on the dodge, your mind starts playing tricks on you. I knew I would go crazy if I didn't return home and kill Tooter Trimble.

There's a thrill in hunting a man, I won't deny that. It sets your blood to tingling and pricks your senses. The closer I got to home, the more my skin crawled with anticipation. Even though it was the hard heat of summer when I neared home, I changed from my regular riding clothes to my wedding suit, covering it with the duster that Pa had been wearing when the Trimbles ambushed him. I checked the load in my revolver and carbine a hundred times. I also kept Snakey's smaller pistol in the pocket of my duster.

I crossed into Palo Pinto County by night and wanted to see the old home place, even if it was foolish. I followed familiar trails, a late-rising full moon making my travel easier until I reached home. I was sorry I'd come. It was desolate, lonely, not like the place I'd grown up in. The charred timbers of the house and barn were all that remained. That and the graves.

I rode to the tree where my family was buried, angering that someone had pulled up the wooden markers and tossed them aside. The dirt on the graves had settled and weeds had taken over, a couple thorny ones reaching up to my stirrup. I dismounted and pulled the taller weeds, then circled around the graves until I found the markers. I pushed them into the ground, wondering how long they would stand before some vandal rode by again. Then, I took off my hat and said a little prayer. That seemed the right thing, the only thing, to do. When I finished, I replaced my hat.

As I mounted, curiosity took hold of me again and I headed toward the Trimble place, even if I was risking trouble. I followed the trail, figuring I'd be less suspicious on the road than slipping through the trees. I gave a loose rein to Pal, letting him save his strength. It lifted my spirit when I found the Trimble place as desolate as Barton land. The barn was standing, but the fire I had started had destroyed the house. The fields were fallow. I wished I knew where the Trimbles were buried so I could spit on their graves and uproot their markers.

I rode away and hid out the following days, avoiding the main trails and any people I saw. I didn't want word to get out I was back. For days I lived off the game I could shoot, regretting every time I killed for food because that was one less bullet I could pump into Tooter Trimble. I laid in wait by back roads on the chance that I would encounter Tooter. Nothing worked, so, every few days, I would circle by the old Trimble place, figuring one day I might see him or his ma. I never did.

Growing weary of hunting a quarry I never found, I became careless and was poking around the Trimble place one morning, not paying attention to things around me. I saw Pal's ears flinch and then stand up. Twisting in my saddle, I saw a half dozen men coming down the trail from the home place. Rangers! They stopped and stared, Henry Brooks yelling at me. I didn't linger for him to repeat his invitation. Slapping Pal with my reins, I bolted away, the Rangers on my tail.

They fired a few shots, the bullets whizzing overhead, but I didn't return any fire, and they quit shooting. It became a horse race. Pal was strong and fast, but the Rangers had good mounts, too. I cursed my carelessness and the long life it had assured Tooter Trimble.

The Rangers stayed on my tail, never really gaining on me. At one time I thought I was pulling away from them, but I was mistaken. Pal was good, but he'd been ridden hard a lot over the last year and wouldn't outlast them. I studied the country flying by me and realized I was galloping toward Dunker Bend and Chicken Shelby's. Seemed kind of ironic that I would get caught where all my troubles had started.

That was when God intervened, by jehu. As I raced into the clearing where the dance had been, I saw a newly whitewashed building and a dozen buggies and maybe four times that many horses. It was the new church. I rode straight there, jumping off Pal and tying him to a buggy as the Rangers broke into the clearing. Pulling a kerchief from my pocket, I wiped the sweat from my face and ran around to the door just as the Rangers neared. I took a deep breath, shoving the kerchief in my duster pocket over Snakey's pistol, and marched inside.

Who should be leading the singing but the preacher himself. His arms were in the air pulsating to the melody when I walked in, but they fell to his side and his face went pale when he saw me. The singing stopped and the men and women sitting on the stiff benches turned, a couple brown-headed boys pointing at me. Behind me I heard a Ranger giving orders and others cocking their guns. I stayed in the open door a moment, my hands sliding to my gunbelt, slowly unbuckling it and letting it slide to the floor. I could feel the aims of the Rangers' guns bearing into my back. My hands rose slowly to take off my hat. Then, I stepped down the aisle.

That was when I saw him.

Tooter Trimble!

And beside him, Ma Trimble on the second row. Damn them!

I stopped about the fifth row and motioned that I wanted a seat. Everybody on the row squeezed toward the wall as if they were afraid of me. Then I lowered myself on the bench, my joints still aching from the chase, my muscles taut with the tension, my mind reeling with my helplessness. Tooter Trimble was sitting not twelve feet from me, looking warily over his shoulder at me, and I couldn't shoot him for fear of harming innocent folk. The Rangers were waiting at the door, and I noticed a couple had taken places by the open windows at each side of the church, blocking what little summer breeze seemed to be coming through.

Collecting his courage, the preacher resumed his singing, but his voice seemed to crack on each line of "Rock of Ages." About me, folks took to singing, cautiously at first, then more recklessly when they realized I wasn't gonna shoot them for missing a note.

After the singing, the preacher passed the hat, fleecing his flock of their hard-scrabble dollars, exhorting them to give so they could one day have a church piano. Mostly, I just stared at Tooter, wishing I had encountered him somewhere else. Alone!

Once, Tooter flicked a fly away from his right ear with his forefinger. I swallowed hard. That was the finger that had killed my wife. My eyes began to water.

About then the preacher began his sermon. He shouted and ranted about smiting evil, crushing it as you would the head of a snake. And I remembered the snake that killed Betsey and how a Trimble had planted it in the gunnysack. The tears in my eyes began to run down my cheeks.

Up front, the preacher realized I was getting emotional and smiled for the first time since I'd entered. He must've thought it was the power of his preaching, because he loosened up and shouted even louder, enjoying God's power he was working over me.

"Smite the evil that's in this world!" he cried.

I just kept nodding through the tears, thinking of Mary Lou and my shattered happiness.

"You are a soldier of the Savior, put on this earth to fight evil," he ranted, really into it.

Some of his words cut through my haze, but mostly I saw Mary Lou dead and her killer sitting almost within reach. And me, I was fighting the tears streaming down my dust-stained face, occasionally pulling the kerchief from my duster pocket to wipe away my grief.

It didn't seem to take as long as one of the preacher's regular sermons, me being in such a haze, but my mind cleared some when folks rose to sing a final hymn, the invitation, as the preacher called it.

"Now come forward and accept Jesus as your Lord," he said. "Together you can fight evil together."

When the singing started, I was standing with the others. I've heard that God works in mysterious ways, and he certainly did that day. No way could I get at Tooter Trimble where he was without spilling innocent blood. But Tooter did a foolish thing. Turning and staring at me for a moment with his crossed eyes, he left his bench for the aisle and marched toward the preacher.

"A soul for God!" the preacher shouted as he took Tooter's hand and shook it briskly. "Amen!"

There he was, Mary Lou's killer, standing before me, before the church, and before God, like a pious saint. He wasn't a convert, just a coward, too scared to give me the same chance at his back that he'd had at mine and Mary Lou's.

I took to sobbing and then did a thing that surprised me more than anyone else in the church. I stepped into the aisle and marched toward the preacher, crying like a fool as I went. Tooter watched me warily with his crossed eyes. I reached into my duster pocket for the kerchief. Tooter's eyes were big as washtubs as my hand reappeared. When he saw I held a kerchief, a slight smile washed across his face, like a man triumphant. Wiping my eyes clear, I nodded at some words the preacher had said, not understanding a thing, and slipped my kerchief into my duster pocket, my fingers wrapping around Snakey's pistol.

"Brethren," the preacher intoned, "we have just witnessed a miracle. Two men from feuding clans washing themselves in the cleansing blood of our Savior and His forgiveness."

A relieved smile was working its way across Tooter's face as he lifted his hand to shake mine. I stared at his forefinger as his hand came waist high. The trigger finger that had killed my wife. Slowly, my hand withdrew from my duster pocket, the duster that Pa had been wearing when a Trimble killed him.

When the revolver cleared cloth, Tooter Trimble froze.

The preacher was still bragging on his power of God when my first shot punctuated his final sentence. My eyes were clear by then, and the bullet struck Tooter in the stomach. I fired again and again, two bullets hitting him in the chest. He staggered toward me, his knees buckling beneath him. Women and kids screamed and men dove for me, knocking over benches as others scrambled for the door. The preacher stepped toward me, but I jumped astride Tooter and fired a fourth and fifth shot into his twitching body.

Then I twisted around and let the preacher look down the barrel of my revolver. He was staring at it, eye to eye, when I pulled the trigger. The gun snapped harmlessly in my hand. The bullet had misfired. I jerked the trigger two more times, but my gun was empty. That probably saved my life, him surviving.

All about me, things were a whirl of movement

and noise—the preacher retreating into a corner, Henry Brooks climbing in through a window, everyone screaming, Ma Trimble sprawling across her dead son. I ran toward an open window, diving through it head first. The ground came up hard to greet me, knocking the empty gun from my hand. On hands and knees I scrambled toward Pal. He was fighting against the tied reins when I reached him.

I heaved for a lungful of air, then loosened the reins and jumped upon his back. He dashed toward freedom with me hunkered low on his back and kicking his flank. Pal got a good start, but before we reached cover I heard gunshots, and his step faltered and his legs buckled beneath him. Hit by a bullet, Pal crumpled to his knees, leaned forward, then fell over as I jumped clear. I landed on my feet and spun around to hide behind Pal. I reached for the carbine in the saddle scabbard and jerked it free. At the church, the Rangers mounted and charged for me, Henry Brooks in the lead. I drew a bead on Henry and came within a hair of pulling the trigger.

But there had been enough killing!

I threw the carbine down and stood up, my hands over my head. Those were my last seconds of freedom for more than fifty years. At least Tooter Trimble was dead and in hell with his kin. I had avenged Mary Lou's death.

That was the end of the feud. A lot of grief had come to pass over some chicken droppings on a new saddle.

There's not much more, other than the trial. This young lawyer from Weatherford, Rutherford S. Simpson, defended me and became famous. He was talented, but, everyone agreed, me included, that I was headed for the hangman. I'd killed a man in church before sixty or so men, women, and children.

Simpson was a tall, lean man with alert eyes and a habit of stroking his chin when he was deep in thought. During my trial, he stroked his chin a lot. He had a resonant voice that demanded respect and an unshakable confidence in himself.

The trial was in August, and the Palo Pinto County Courthouse was as hot as the emotions inside it. As the last surviving Barton man, I wasn't liked. I never could figure out why the Trimbles were more popular, but Simpson fought public emotion the whole trial. Except for Simpson, Momma, and the Russell family, no one favored me at the trial.

The prosecutor, a small man with big political aspirations, figured to claim a seat in the Texas legislature by sending me to the gallows. The trial in the early going was pretty much as you would expect, the prosecutor calling witness after witness, including some of the Rangers that had seen the shooting. All agreed I'd shot Tooter, but Simpson kept making my plight worse by asking each witness if I had been crying. I was embarrassed.

It took three days for the prosecutor to make it through all his witnesses, his smile growing bigger each time a finger was pointed at me. Simpson kept stroking his chin and not doing much else, except asking every witness if he'd seen tears in my eyes. The third afternoon of the trial, the prosecutor called the preacher, making him his last witness. The preacher testified with glee, but Simpson didn't question him that day, it being late, and the judge adjourning for the day. I figured by winter I'd be dead and buried like my loved ones.

When the preacher took the stand the next day, Rutherford S. Simpson began his defense before God, judge, and jury. He said he would call no defense witnesses, but he did have a few questions for the preacher.

"Many fine, honorable folk have testified against Clements Barton, my client, and I'll not dispute their testimony," he began to the hush of the courtroom. "Who can dispute the testimony under oath of some of Palo Pinto County's most law-abiding citizens? Who can dispute the testimony under oath of the fine Rangers who returned law and order to the county?"

I could almost feel the prickle of the hemp around my neck, not that I cared with Mary Lou dead, but I didn't want Ma Trimble to have the satisfaction of watching me hang.

"No one can dispute it," Simpson continued, "but one man, respected by all in this room, can show you that Clements Barton is not the cold-blooded killer that you have been led to believe. That man is the man who delivered the sermon the day Tooter Trimble was shot, the man on the witness stand before us."

The spectators gasped, then took to murmuring, until the judge gaveled them to order. I sank in my hard chair, the shackles rattling on my feet. To think my life depended on the testimony of a man I hated as bad as any Trimble troubled me.

On the stand, the preacher seemed confident, though his eyes narrowed at Simpson, then focused on the prosecutor, who answered him with a shrug and a frown that suggested he might be worried about that seat in the legislature.

Then, Simpson began to stalk the preacher. "Now Reverend, do you consider yourself a good preacher, a man who can stir people's emotions"—Simpson paused for a moment—"to the glory of God, of course?" Simpson turned away before the preacher nodded. "I didn't hear you," Simpson said.

"Yes, sir," the preacher answered sharply.

"Everyone has agreed my client, Clements Barton, was tearful during your sermon. You have such a way with words—can you do that to people regularly, working through the power of God, of course, Reverend?"

"Well, yes," the preacher replied, suspicion growing in his cold eyes.

"You expounded upon smiting out evil the day of the shooting, did you not?"

The preacher stared hard at Simpson, not liking the way he was headed. "Yes," he again answered, "but—"

Simpson held his hand up for silence, and the rest of the preacher's explanation died on his lips.

"Did he take aim at you the day of the shooting?"

"He did indeed," the preacher answered triumphantly, "but the gun misfired."

"An act of God, might you say?" Simpson held up his hand like he expected no answer. "Did Clements Barton shoot at anybody else besides you and the deceased Trimble lad?"

The preacher shrugged, then smiled. "I wasn't keeping up with all his shooting."

"No one else has said so. In fact, the Rangers have acknowledged he never fired at them; even when his horse was downed and he had his carbine, he tossed it aside. They even say he left his gunbelt lying on the church floor." Simpson eyed the preacher coldly. "Evil? A terrible concept, difficult to define, wouldn't you say?"

"God knows evil and it's here on this earth," the preacher interjected. "It's as plain as black and white."

"To God it is, Reverend, but man is not as wise as God. At least I am not. Are you?"

The spectators laughed at the preacher. That pleased me, especially when the preacher shook his red face.

"Why," Simpson continued, "would Clements Barton shoot at you and Hezekiah Trimble alone of all the people in the church, alone of all the Rangers outside the church? Why would he want to shoot the man who had married him?"

The preacher shrugged. "Ask him."

"I don't have to, Reverend, because I know. Did you tell anyone that you were going to marry Clements Barton to Mary Lou Russell? Think about it very carefully, Reverend. Remember you are under oath before the God you serve. Did you?"

Sinking into his chair, the reverend paled. Behind me, I heard the squeak of benches as spectators leaned forward to hear his reply. Then, with great effort, he nodded.

"I didn't hear you, Reverend."

"Yes, yes, I told someone."

"Who?"

"Ma Trimble," he replied. The audience gasped. "I told her he planned to marry and leave Texas. Then her boy Hezekiah wouldn't have to live in fear as he had since the feud started."

Simpson nodded. "Do you know who killed Mary Lou Russell Barton?"

The preacher nodded weakly. "Hezekiah Trimble came to me asking if God could forgive him for killing Mary Lou. He said he meant to kill Clem, but his aim was awry."

"And he knew when and where he could ambush Clem because you'd violated God's trust and told the Trimbles they would be leaving for New Mexico Territory after the wedding?"

The preacher's head drooped and his voice could barely be heard, even in the hush. "Yes."

"You are as much at fault as Clements Barton for Hezekiah Trimble's death. Instead of teaching the compassion of Jesus, you sowed the hatred and vengeance of the Old Testament." Simpson paused, letting his silence prick the preacher. "Clements Barton killed Tooter Trimble," Simpson began, "I shall not deny that. But he did it in self-defense against a man who'd backshot his wife and might backshoot him. And the man who had betrayed Clements Barton had betrayed his plans as surely as Judas Iscariot betrayed Christ our Savior, and that man is the one who delivered that sermon the day Hezekiah Trimble was shot. Yes, the Reverend's finger, too, was around the trigger that killed Hezekiah Trimble."

Then Simpson turned away from the devastated preacher and faced the jury. "Gentlemen, I do not ask you to ignore what my client has done. I ask only that you show him more mercy than has been shown him by this man of God." Simpson came back to the table and placed his hand on my shoulder. "I rest my defense," he said.

The jury was out thirty minutes, returning with a guilty verdict. But, instead of the gallows, they sentenced me to fifty years in prison. The papers wrote up Simpson's masterful defense and gave him a courtroom reputation he would embellish for years.

There's not much else to my story. I hadn't been in prison more than two years when I got a letter saying the preacher had died under mysterious circumstances that left folks wondering whether it had been a suicide or a murder.

Fifty years in prison doesn't make much more of a story, though I never felt right in here, not with all those murderers. I was just fending for myself and never took anything more than Snakey's ten dollars and his pistol. That and the lives of the Trimble men, but they weren't worth nothing.

Warden John Warrenberg shook his head at the end of Clements Barton's story. The long afternoon shadows made it hard to be certain, but Warrenberg thought he saw tears running down the old man's cheeks.

Henry Brooks reached over from his chair and patted Barton's hand. Barton nodded, then wiped at the corner of his eyes.

"You'll be okay?" the old Ranger asked.

Barton shrugged. "It don't matter. Nothing's been okay since the social at Dunker Bend."

The Ranger shook his head. "I knew you could've killed me when we captured you, Clem, but I didn't realize you could've shot me when I visited your momma. Guess I owe you double what I thought."

"No, sir, we're even. You could've shot me when I stood in the church door."

Brooks shook his head. "We thought we had you when you dropped your gunbelt and we didn't want to risk hitting innocent people."

"I didn't set out to kill innocent folks either, Henry, just the Trimbles. Us Bartons weren't bad folks, never meant to be. It was just that things got out of hand, and all of it over a piece of horse jewelry."

Barton lifted his left hand and pointed at his ring finger.

The warden could just make out a tiny braided band around the wrinkled flesh of his finger.

"It's all I got left from Mary Lou," he said toying with the braided band. "It's the hair Momma clipped from her head and braided for me. I've managed to keep it all these years to remind me of her. It's that and memories, that's all I've got left. Not a day has passed since she died that I haven't thought of her, wishing things had turned out differently."

Warrenberg didn't know what to say. He felt sorry for the old man, but words seemed so inadequate after what Clements Barton had been through. By Warrenberg's count six Bartons, eight Trimbles, a sheriff, and Mary Lou had died. Before him sat two men separated yet bound by fifty years and sixteen deaths.

"I told you the truth as I remember it," Barton said.

Henry Brooks nodded. "I'm sorry about Mary Lou."

Barton turned to the Ranger. "Why didn't you come to her funeral to arrest me?"

"Same reason I didn't shoot you at the church. We feared innocent folks might get killed. Too, a man, no matter his kind, should be allowed to mourn his wife."

Barton bit his lip, and Warrenberg thought he was about to start crying.

"I figure you've got a lot of regrets, Clem, losing Mary Lou and all."

Barton nodded. "Many, many after losing Mary Lou and my family, but one above all the others."

"What would that be?" Brooks asked leaning forward in his chair.

At the question, Barton began to cry. He tried to say something, then just sobbed.

Brooks reached over and patted his hand again.

It was several minutes before Barton spoke again. "Most of all—" he started and paused, his eyes closing for several seconds, then finally opening again. "Most of all, I wish Tooter and I'd never wiped those chicken droppings on Vernon's saddle."